<oaicite:5555100:0000000000000000000000000000000000000000000000000000000000000000PRAISE FOR

ANOXIA

"Set on the storm-lashed Mediterranean coast, *Anoxia* is a
powerful, atmospheric novel that explores grief, art, and the
transformative power of creation. As floodwaters reshape
the land, Dolores—paralyzed by the loss of her husband—
seeks solace in the lost art of daguerreotype photography,
which captures not just a tangible image, but the shimmering
essence of a moment in time. Dolores begins working with a
mysterious older man who collects postmortem images, and
learns that by capturing death, she is, paradoxically, reclaiming
her own life. In this luminous novel, we follow the story of her
awakening. A daringly original novel by one of the most gifted
writers of the vibrant contemporary Spanish scene, *Anoxia* is
a gorgeous meditation on the human experience, where art
becomes both a vessel for grief and a source of profound,
transformational beauty."

—Valerie Miles, author of
A Thousand Forests in One Acorn

"Today, the old art of portraying the dead is disappearing. This
novel is a powerful creation that draws on both the materiality of photography and the enigmas of death. Photography is
different from the images of our digital age, and its outcome—
memory—deals as much with the past as with the present.
Death, the source of our work of mourning, does not simply
mean loss, since it engenders a new relationship with the

dead, who continue haunting our lives. With *Anoxia*, Walter Benjamin, Roland Barthes, and Susan Sontag have found a literary companion capable of dialoguing with them. An amazing accomplishment."

—Enzo Traverso, author of *Gaza Faces History*

"Miguel Ángel Hernández writes novels that integrate a gripping fabula with one or more important theoretical issues. While reading the engaging story, the reader cannot help but absorb relevant ideas about social-political reality as well as aesthetic questions. The literary quality matches the level of thinking. In *Anoxia* this concerns the combination of the art of photography with the personal effort of memory. Once you read all his novels you will have acquired unique insights that are indispensable but difficult to learn through teaching and studying."

—Mieke Bal, author of *Narratology* and *Quoting Caravaggio*

"An enthralling story about photography, and the limits between life and death."

—*ABC Cultural*

"In *Anoxia*...[Hernández] has achieved the perfect equilibrium...The tradition of mortuary photography drives a mysterious plot that flirts with the thriller, though the greatest value lies in the subtlety with which Hernández tackles the emotional consequences of grief."

—*El Cultural*

ANOXIA

ANOXIA

MIGUEL ÁNGEL HERNÁNDEZ

Translated from the Spanish
by Adrian Nathan West

• • •

OTHER PRESS
NEW YORK

Originally published in Spanish as *Anoxia* in 2023
by Editorial Anagrama, Barcelona
Copyright © Miguel Ángel Hernández, 2023
Translation copyright © Other Press, 2025
Published in agreement with Casanovas & Lynch Literary Agency

Title-page image provided by Shutterstock,
contributed by Wichan Kongchan

Production editor: Yvonne E. Cárdenas
Text designer: Patrice Sheridan
This book was set in Adobe Caslon and Agenda by
Alpha Design & Composition of Pittsfield, NH

1 3 5 7 9 10 8 6 4 2

Library of Congress Cataloging-in-Publication Data
Names: Hernández, Miguel Ángel, 1977- author. |
West, Adrian Nathan, translator.
Title: Anoxia : a novel / Miguel Ángel Hernández ; translated from
the Spanish by Adrian Nathan West.
Other titles: Anoxia. English
Description: New York : Other Press, 2025.
Identifiers: LCCN 2024023368 (print) | LCCN 2024023369 (ebook) |
ISBN 9781635424584 (paperback) | ISBN 9781635424591 (ebook)
Subjects: LCSH: Death—Fiction. | Postmortem photography—Fiction. |
LCGFT: Psychological fiction. | Novels.
Classification: LCC PQ6708.E765 A7513 2025 (print) |
LCC PQ6708.E765 (ebook) | DDC 863/.7—dc23/eng/20240520
LC record available at https://lccn.loc.gov/2024023368
LC ebook record available at https://lccn.loc.gov/2024023369

Publisher's Note

FOR RAQUEL,
ETERNALLY ON THIS SIDE

I have wondered sometimes whether eternity might not after all exist as the endless prolongation of the moment of death...

—GRAHAM GREENE, *THE END OF THE AFFAIR*

I

THE LAST IMAGE

. . .

1

SHE TRIES TO LOOK AT THE DEAD MAN THROUGH the viewfinder alone. He's in front of her, but her eyes are fixed on the image formed through the lines: the coppery glow of the wooden coffin, bony hands intertwined on the chest, golden ring on the ring finger, suit charcoal gray, shirt white, tie black, with silver stripes, face lifeless. The pale surface of the skin, like marble, reflecting the light, forcing her to move the camera, and move it again, until she finds the perfect angle.

The cold in the small room in the funeral home bristles the hair on Dolores's hefty body. She should have brought a coat, or at least a shawl to cover her shoulders and the slender silk of her blouse. She didn't think before she left home, and now she regrets it. The aluminum tripod turned freezing as soon as she entered, and the camera is like a block of ice. She can feel it when she rests her cheek on it to check the image through the metal viewfinder. After deliberation, she chose the Nikon F4. It's more than twenty years old and heavy as an anvil, but she likes it, she feels comfortable with it. And it was Luis's favorite. For some reason, that, too, affected her choice.

She's not alone there. The daughter of the deceased, in customary black, is accompanying her in silence. She can't be too much older. Sixty, maybe. Dolores feels her inquisitive gaze with every small movement she makes. But still, she prefers being watched to remaining alone with the body.

Her movements are silent, slow, and respectful. Her voice is hardly audible as she asks for permission to move the flowers to clear her line of sight. She pushes aside the wreaths and places the tripod at the proper distance. She's trying to be quick, and to focus on her work, knowing that her time there is borrowed, and she's interrupting an act of mourning. And every slight shift, every minimal click of the shutter, recalls to her the discomfort of the woman there scrutinizing her with a vexation made evident no sooner than she'd entered:

"I'm respecting this, because it's my father's wishes," she said in a dry tone, with a sour expression, before the worker opened the room for the viewing. "But this is a fixation of that crazy old man. So please, hurry up and get it over with."

The crazy old man. Her words give form—however vague—to the voice that is the origin of all this. The phone call. Yesterday, late in the afternoon. A grave timbre, an accent she couldn't identify. And the commission—the plea, rather—the strangest one she has ever received in all her days as a photographer.

"My friend died," the voice said. "I promised him one last photo."

For a few seconds, Dolores was unsure how to respond. A photo of a dead man? Was this some kind of joke? But the tone left no room for doubt. The caller was serious. He'd planned to do it himself, he said, but he'd had an accident at home and couldn't leave. He would pay whatever she asked. And it wouldn't be difficult: a few shots of the body, however she thought best, but only in black and white. If she could load the camera with Tri-X 400, all the better: not too grainy, and sensitive enough for a poorly lit space. The one thing was, he said, it was pressing. She would need to arrive early. Before the funeral. The very next morning.

After hanging up, she needed a few minutes to think. She hadn't shot in black and white for years, but she still had some on the shelf in her storage room she could use if it hadn't expired. She'd never done anything like this. With Luis, she'd covered everything: baptisms, weddings, communions, celebrations, she even photographed a traffic accident at the request of the local police. But a dead man...she'd never done any*thing* like that.

And she still isn't sure why she said yes the afternoon before. Perhaps it was the sense that he was begging her. Or because, for the first time in ages, she felt she could be useful, and that photography, at least in this instance, meant something again. Or maybe it was just an impulse, and she'd said yes the same way she might have said no. But she thinks there's always a hidden reason to everything. She doesn't know how to formulate it, but it's what brought her there now, to the local funeral home, in front of a stranger's body, observing his face attentively through the viewfinder, trying to concentrate, feeling on her neck the impatient gaze of the woman in mourning. The cold has crept into her body, and she has gooseflesh on her arms.

When she leaves, the early August heat greets her. She stands a few seconds in the doorway, sheltered in the shadows of the redbrick walls. It's just a bay in an industrial park on the outskirts of the village. Far off, the sea. She feels the breeze, smells the slight aroma of salt, tries and fails to fill her lungs and exhales the undigested perfume of flowers and sterility that lives inside her now.

As she tries to breathe, she sees familiar faces looking at her. She noticed them when she went inside. But she prefers not to go over to them, not to ask. She doesn't want to know anything about the person she's photographed. Their pain isn't hers. It doesn't concern her. Not now.

She walks to the white Corsa and leaves her camera and tripod in the backseat. She moves like an automaton, trying not to think of other funeral homes, another time, other dead.

Before turning the key, she checks the rearview to make sure there are no cars behind her. From inside it, the furrows and spots on her skin, her sunken eyelids, look back at her, the curls of her hair gone gray and never dyed since. In a few months, she'll be fifty-nine, but her face has lived several lives. Three, at least, in the last decade.

She tries not to look at the passenger seat, but she senses the dark absence there, the hollowness that has accompanied her for some time. It's dense today, and hazy, and sucks up the air around it. She has to lower her window and stick her head out to breathe.

In her mind, the words of the dead man's daughter echo.

That crazy old man, she keeps thinking.

This crazy old woman, she says to herself.

2

SHE'S STILL ASKING HERSELF WHY SHE AC-
cepted the job as, careful not to hurt her back, she lifts
the rolling blind and pushes the door to the shop.

She didn't rush down. It's after eleven, but most
likely not a single customer has come by that morning.
The shop—the studio, as she prefers to call it—has long
ceased to be what it was. Only a few people come past to
buy film or develop it, or to print their digital photos—
that never did catch on. A few sentimental souls. Lately,
people don't even need photos for their IDs. You can
do everything from home now. That's probably why the
special events business dried up too. Everyone's got a
camera on their phone. And of course everyone thinks
they're a photographer.

Shut it down. You don't need it. Teresa, Luis's sister,
tells her that all the time. She's right. With what she gets
from her savings and renting out the summer house she
inherited from her parents, she makes enough to mud-
dle through and even pay for Iván's school. There's not

much left, but she knows how to manage it. Her family home is two blocks from the beach, three bedrooms and a small enclosed patio. She started renting it out after her mother died, when her father was sick and alone and they decided he should come live with them outside of town, where you could no longer see the sea.

Now, ten years after Luis's death and almost five years after her father's, she could sell it. But renting it is enough. Anyway, despite the transformations, despite its camouflage of Ikea furniture, it's still the house she was born in, the one where she spent half her life. She can't get rid of it. Just like she can't close the shop. Luis is still there. More than anywhere else.

They opened the shop in 1990, the same year they were married. They invested everything they had. L&L, they called it. Luis and Lola. *L and L!* he said jovially, and clapped his hands like a flamenco player, the day they put the logo on the door. That studio was their future, their life project. Now it's their past.

They bought the two-story house and turned the bottom floor into the studio. The first year, they spent more time downstairs than up. Dolores came to think maybe they didn't need the living space.

They were lucky from the start. Luis had experience shooting special occasions and was known in the villages on the coast. When he went out on his own, he took his clients with him. The nineties were good years. Especially for photo albums. They did marriages, communions, and baptisms for half the coast. Then, all at once, everyone decided they were a photographer and didn't need professionals anymore.

Luis saw it coming. But he assumed it would pass. People would return to cameras, film, and real photographers. They'd realize they'd made a mistake. All the two of them needed was to hold tight. Wait for everything to go back to the way it should be. They'd be back. Sooner or later. Luis was wrong. No one came back. And neither did the old days.

They got a photo printer, started selling memory cards and digital cameras. But that only worked a few years. Luis was right when he said everything was moving too fast and it was impossible to keep up. You've got to stop somewhere, he said. Find a fixed point and stay there.

She did. Or rather, that point found her: that instant in which the world started moving at top speed and she stopped running behind it. She doesn't have to think too hard to find it. It's not abstract, it's marked in time. A cut. A caesura that divides a world—her world—in two. One part that advances, one that remains immobile. She remembers the year, the month, the day, the hour. That instant is burnt into her memory. Thursday, March 26, 2009, at seven thirty at night. The call echoing through the room. The voice announcing the accident. The pain. The guilt. The origin of the dark absence that has accompanied her ever since.

Ten years have passed. And though the world hasn't stopped moving—her son Iván has grown, and much has changed—she's still where she was then, developing a few rolls of film a month and doing a couple of budget shoots a year, a dull echo of what she'd managed in the past.

She could close the studio and take her sister-in-law's advice. Sure. But holding out there is what's kept her afloat, even as her movements resemble those of a cartoon character who's run off a cliff and is still kicking his feet until he realizes there's no more ground beneath him. Inertia. That's what defines her: rolling the blinds up each day, wiping the glass counter, holding on to the stacks of film spread across the shelves, checking their expiration dates, negotiating with suppliers, standing there, day after day, as though the ground hadn't crumbled away one afternoon in 2009, as though she could still touch that time from before, which from one day to the next exploded and has never been put back together again.

3

FOR DAYS, DOLORES THINKS SHE'S BEEN DE-
ceived. A sick joke, she tells herself. No one answers the
landline the studio received that call from, and no one
comes to inquire about the photos. It's not the money
that matters; it wasn't much of a loss. It's not the time: at
least she filled it with something. But it bothers her that
no one's gotten in touch, and all week she can't clear the
worry from her head. She wakes up with it every morning and it won't go away, even on her daily walks to the
esplanade.

Fifty minutes there and back. Rain or shine. In summer, she gets up at dawn to avoid the heat and the tourists. She's lived with them since she was born and sees
them as just another part of the landscape, but she can't
help feeling a pinprick of rage when the good weather
comes and their presence shatters the tranquility of the
village.

When she was a girl, she hated them. She's never
known why, if it's because they poached her secret places

or because they abandoned her just before fall. Every year, the same thing. Friends who came and vanished. And then came back the next summer and expected her to still be there, like a tree, a fixture, along with the boats, the deck chairs, the cabanas. Perennial, like her parents' bar, which also filled up in the warm months.

After her First Communion, Dolores started *helping out* there, as her father said. On the weekends and in the summers. She still hasn't forgotten. The racket still sounds in her ears. The noise, the shouts. She hears them from her home, just a few yards from the bar. The violent report of the dominoes, the drained wineglasses on metal tables, the chairs dragged around, the tumult of televised soccer... and in particular the voices of men. Because only men went to her father's bar. For women, it was a foreign country. Whenever one of them crossed the tinsel curtain unawares, especially in summer, the men's eyes settled on her body like a swarm of bees. Dolores remembers when she started feeling them: the stares held too long, double-edged remarks. Here, gorgeous. My, you've grown. That's the kind of service I like. Bring me a nip of wine, honey, but you bring it yourself, you're easier on the eyes than your old man. Then the tips. Arm held on to a little longer than was proper. Rough hands on taut skin. Forced smile concealing disgust.

Her father must have noticed at some point, and that's what made him decide her place wasn't behind the bar or waiting tables before the eyes of all, but in the kitchen, making tapas and meals. She'd be safe there. Far from the noise, she thought. But the din crept through the window inside and echoed cruelly between those four walls. It still isn't gone, not completely. It comes back sometimes, like an unintelligible murmur, a purring of the past growing louder in her ears.

Maybe that's why she yearns for silence. She has ever since then. Silence and calm. The serenity of the placid sea. She never liked the summer, but she likes the sea. The small sea where she was born. Europe's largest salt-water lake, the lagoon known by all as the Mar Menor, which means *the lesser sea*. Still, serene, its far edge visible on the horizon. The more years passed, the more she was struck by the way her gaze held it. Like a photograph, almost. Nothing lies outside your field of vision in the Mar Menor. There is no beyond for the eye to get lost in. That distinguishes it from the immensity of the open seas, which has always unsettled her. The loss of limits. Spilling over. And so she likes this sea, trimmed to the scale of her vision. She feels she can possess it, that it belongs to her. That may well be why the tourists have always irked her. They take from her a place of her own she doesn't want to share.

She likes walking early, before the sun's really shining. It does her weary body good, but her head most of all. She started doing it after Luis died. She needed it. The walking and the silence. She'd leave her phone at home and stroll among the whispers of the still-sleeping village. She still does that today, and it's the only thing that comforts her, her little walk and the breeze caressing her face and that instant of serenity, that moment of repose when she reaches the beach. Resting her back against one of the benches on the esplanade, eyes trying to take possession of the limits of that tiny sea. Alone. Calm. Quiet. A brief interlude of permanence. Even the dark absence that accompanies her seems to give her space.

At the end of the week, the phone rings. A man's voice again, deep and husky, with an odd accent she doesn't recognize. Clemente Artés, he says. Yes, Clemente. She wrote the name on a piece of paper, but she can't stop calling him *the old man*. That's how she's imagined him these past few days. She can't get the daughter's comment out of her head.

"I'm sorry I didn't call before."

"I thought you'd disappeared."

He apologizes again. He tells her he's gone to physical therapy several mornings in a row, and that's why no one was home to answer the phone.

"As you can imagine, rehabbing a hip is a long and complicated process."

This time she apologizes for her lack of consideration. She tells him she took ten photos or more, and asks if he wants all of them. She doesn't tell him the film expired years ago and she's worried the image might be faded.

"I want them all," he says. "The contact sheet too. I'll ask to have a few blown up later, probably into nine by sevens."

He seems to know what he's talking about. Dolores tells him she'll have them developed in a couple of days.

"I'll send someone to pick them up. I'm still not mobile. And I'll pay, of course, too. If you tell me what I owe you."

Dolores has been thinking this over. On their first call, he'd said money wasn't an issue. But she'll try to be fair. She'll charge for travel time, her hourly, plus materials. But nothing extra for the short notice or the unusual commission. Or the insomnia, the nerves, the discomfort. She wouldn't know how to put a price on that.

That same afternoon, she shuts herself up in the darkroom to develop the film. There, she pays attention to the dead man for the first time. This, for her, is the heart of photography, the moment when the image emerges like a ghost across time. That's why early on—and Luis agreed—she was determined to buy her own enlarger and start developing herself, even if it was just her own contact sheets and photos. Commissions, commercial work she sent mostly to the lab, but even with them, she felt the occasional need to be there to watch the image being born. She liked the ritual. The sacred silence. The red shadow. The dark, endless evening. Even the scent of fixer clinging to her fingers. She couldn't help bringing the paper to her nose after emptying the trays, breathing in softly and feeling her eyes go damp. Passing her fingertips over her lips, tasting the salinity and testing the roughness of her dry skin, cracking from exposure to chemicals.

Luis hated that, but soon it had become a habit. Put on gloves, please, he told her more than once, after touching the burnt skin on her hands. But she liked the watery feel of it, and the idea that a relic of the image remained somehow on her fingers.

The material aspect of the job interested her husband less. What he liked was the gaze, the frame, the focus, the end result, not what lay behind it—craft, as he liked to call it. He didn't want to get his hands dirty. She didn't mind: for her, the process was inseparable from the end. A painter doesn't just paint, he stretches the canvas, readies his brushes, even frames his work afterward. Luis knew the basics, of course. He just didn't care. Or not as much as she. In the end, she was manning the stoves. He preferred being out there, visible, exhibiting his art to the public.

She remembers the first months after his death. She went to the darkroom and redeveloped all his photos. The portraits, but also the landscapes, the views of the village, the sea. His gaze. She needed to see him appear again.

She spent her mornings and evenings shut inside. She'd close the shop, lower the rolling blind, and hide where she could summon ghosts. A Ouija board of images. A Ouija board for a woman of little faith. If only she could believe in something besides images, she told herself over and over. Because then she could give meaning to this strange absence that had begun taking shape beside her. An invisible hollow that materialized and has followed her ever since. A black hole that periodically turns dense and tangible and sucks up all the air.

She's never told anyone about it. Not even her sister-in-law. Nor is there a reason to. It's just a feeling, after all. And one she wouldn't know how to explain. The constant intuition of a blind spot in space, a breakdown, a drain her oxygen escapes through. More absence than presence. The inverse of a ghost. A palpable breach that is always there, even when she can't see it.

Ten years have passed, and Dolores doesn't shut herself away as she did before. But the absence is still there with her. Sometimes she hardly notices it, she even manages to forget it. Other times, it grows so solid it can nearly touch her. And yet she still believes in nothing but photography. The power of images to resuscitate the past. That's the only ghost they can convoke. And so the figure that appeared when she developed her film today hardly left an impression on her. It's a dead man, nothing more. A soulless body that looks like it's asleep. Granted a bit of life, maybe, by the photo. That does surprise her. The life of the image. The life things take on when they're captured by the camera. The way inert objects in photos seem to pause, as if frozen briefly in their transit toward elsewhere.

This is how the dead man's image emerges in contact with the paper. Dormant, listless, but on the verge of waking, moving on, the way life always moves, however much you think it's stopped forever.

4

DESPITE HIS RECEDING HAIRLINE AND HIS somewhat shabby appearance, the man who walks through the shop door can't be over forty. She can tell by the gleam of his smooth, dark skin. Young skin. She always notices that. The way skin reflects light.

"Vasil," he says. "I'm here to pick up photos of Mr. Clemente."

His foreign accent reminds her of someone from a spy movie. She shoots sidelong glances at him as she digs through the drawer under the counter. There's nothing in it but the envelope of photos, but still she takes her time, pretending to push aside other orders. In the meantime, the man takes from his pocket a stack of bills wrapped in a rubber band and places it on the counter.

"Here you are," she says finally.

Before he accepts the photos, he pushes the money toward her.

"Make sure it's all there, please."

Dolores takes off the rubber band and counts the fifteen ten-euro bills.

"Perfect."

The man then takes the envelope of photos, and without opening it drops it into a beige bag with the Kodak logo in the center. He does it slowly, as if unacquainted with haste. Only after this is done does he say:

"Thank you. From Mr. Clemente. It means a lot, he says me to tell you."

That same afternoon, she learns Vasil is Bulgarian and has been taking care of Clemente Artés for months. Artés tells her himself on the phone when he calls to thank her for her work.

"I'd like all of them blown up," he says. "Time's not a worry. There's not a single one I don't like. I can't believe you've never taken this kind of photo before."

"It's experience," she says, "I've been doing this for years."

"There's something to your gaze. A special way of seeing things."

Dolores thanks him for the compliment. The way he pronounces words is striking. Careful but fussy, separating each word from the other. That and his deep voice bring a peculiar solemnity to everything he says.

"I also appreciate your discretion," he continues. "You haven't once asked me anything."

"It's not my business."

"He was a friend of mine, the man in the photos. I promised him I'd capture this last moment. I devoted my life to doing this for others. How could I not do it for him too?"

"Sure," she responds. And she decides to sit in the small chair behind the counter, woven of bulrushes, the one she salvaged from her father's house, which is more comfortable than any fancy armchair.

Artés tells her he used to work as a photographer in France—at last she realizes where his accent's from—and that he retired to the coast several years ago. He took portraits of the dead in Marseille. And though that tradition declined decades ago and is now more or less forgotten, he tried to keep the embers of it alive. He will continue to do so as long as he has his strength. Even if more than a few people may think he's lost his mind.

"The dead aren't invisible," he argues. "Even if nowadays everyone tries to sweep them under the rug. What I do is important, you know? I should have told you all this before."

"I understand," she responds, but she doesn't really know what it is she's supposed to understand.

"You do, don't you, I have the impression you do."

He continues, telling her how he slipped and fell in the shower. He's certain he was lucky, despite everything: he could have hit his head. He tells her about his operation, his physical therapy. The pain. The sleepless nights. But the important thing, he says, is he's started to move around again, and when he can walk, he'd like to come pick up the enlarged photos and speak to her in person.

"It would be a pleasure," Dolores responds.

And as she hangs up, she thinks it will be. A pleasure. There's something in his way of talking that at once unsettles and seduces her. Maybe it's the compliments. *Your gaze. A special way of seeing things.* It's been years since anyone's said anything nice about her. Years since anyone's said anything at all.

5

"I'M INTRIGUED, I WANT TO MEET HIM," SHE
says, after telling Teresa about the call from Clemente
Artés.

Once a week, at least, they meet late in the day for a
talk over drinks. They have since Luis died. Teresa was
determined to get her out of the studio, even if it was
just for a few hours in the afternoon. They'd meet at the
restaurant in the port and carry on about their week and
mourn together. How they'd seen this on TV, how that
had happened in the village, and they'd gripe about the
tourists in summer and rejoice when September came,
as it had just now, and the restaurant turned tranquil
once again.

Dolores thought those moments did her sister-in-law
good, too, maybe even more than they did for her. Teresa
never spoke of her emotions, and behaved as if nothing
had happened. Yet Dolores could see the grief in the
back of her eyes and hear it in the texture of her warbling

voice, which had suddenly deepened, just as her slender body seemed to have shrunk a few inches.

Luis was her older brother and had been like a father to her. Dolores knew Teresa before she knew Luis, and for a long time, he was just her friend's brother. But he had a grown man's body, and she had noticed that right away. A difference of four years is nothing, but for an adolescent, it's an eternity, and it put him, his long blond hair, his shaggy beard, out of her reach. His hair and his height and his stocky build made people mistake him for a Swedish tourist. All that plus the camera he always had around his neck.

"I've got to go, the Viking's here," Teresa used to say when Luis came to pick her up on his motorcycle.

He was always distant when he waved at her. Dolores had wished she could climb onto that bike that made a hellish racket and hold his body tight. She kept this secret at first, but as time went on, she stopped bothering. Still, years passed before Luis noticed her and their destinies crossed. She was a girl, and she couldn't imagine all the things they'd live through together, she and the Viking. The happiness and adventure at first. The pain and sorrow that would come later.

After he died, Dolores tried to revisit those bright memories and experience them again. But the accident blocked her access to the memory of that early joy and painted everything in the same dark tones, the same bitterness. Guilt, remorse, distance. Years had to pass for those memories to return without that sheen of agony, and even still, a shadow hovers over them, the absence that keeps her chained to that afternoon in March when time stopped.

Teresa tried to help her move on. Rebuild her emotional life. Introducing her to friends and acquaintances she's dodged like arrows. Teresa doesn't understand her preference for calm and routine, her shutting herself up in her refuge, her discomfort at the mere idea of dressing up to go pretend she feels something she doesn't. She's at ease in her baggy dresses and her comfortable flats. She doesn't obsess over extra pounds or another inch on her hipline. Or the spots or wrinkles on her face or the ashy color of her curly hair. Every time Teresa's insisted they have lunch or dinner with someone *interesting*— this term is a constant in her vocabulary—Dolores has agreed to put on eyeliner and lipstick at most. The hardest thing has always been faking a smile.

"You and that sour puss of yours," Teresa often ends up saying. "I can't do anything with you."

"You know I can't stand this."

"You're waiting for Richard Gere, Lola, and he's not going to come, that's your problem."

She says that a lot too. Or did, until she got divorced three years ago, and couldn't find anyone she liked either. But she seems to confront solitude differently, like a kind of second youth, uninhibited, with no ties to anything.

Her last years with Paco weren't easy. Dolores never knew them to get along. Teresa called almost every week to tell her about some fight with her husband. The hard-headed bastard, she used to say. Dolores had never really liked him, but she suffered his bluster in silence over family meals. He'd made out like a bandit with a couple of housing developments on the coast, and would boast about his BMWs and the plasma TVs in every room of the house, the bottles of Vega Sicilia he used to open for them.

Luis liked him even less than she did. But he was his brother-in-law, and he tried to put a good face on in his presence. Luis didn't get to witness his decline. The bursting of the bubble. No more pricey cars or good wine. The inability to admit it was over. Dolores blamed herself for seeing it as poetic justice, especially when she saw how it affected her friend, who had to go back to her old job at the health department to try and tame her husband's exorbitant debts. They nearly split up two years after Luis's death, but then, for a while, things got better. Until Paula went off to Granada for college and Rubén started military school. With her children gone, Teresa felt there was no more reason to go home. She'd make up work meetings and stay in Murcia for lunch and even for dinner. The man waiting for her at home was someone she no longer had anything in common with.

She'd never admit it, but Dolores was relieved when they got divorced, because Teresa stopped trying to fix *her* life and concentrated on fixing her own. Dolores became her companion at dinners and in the village. And she was much more comfortable in the roles of observer and, especially, of confidante.

Which is what she feels like now on this Friday in early September, when they meet at a restaurant and Teresa confesses that she's finally found someone who turns her on. He's a dentist, and he's started working with her at the health department. They met at a dinner. He's divorced and has two kids.

"I can't stop thinking about him," she says.

Dolores then tells her about the call from Clemente Artés and says that she's intrigued and wants to meet him. She doesn't tell her that she hasn't been able to get his voice out of her head since she heard it on the phone, or that for a few moments his compliment, unexpected and not quite opportune, made her happy.

"Imagine if he was like an interesting older man— like Indiana Jones's dad?"

Dolores smiles. That's not what she imagines. In reality, she imagines nothing. But she does want the day to come when she can put a face and body to that deep voice and the kind words that have burst into her quiet world.

6

SHE SEES IT ARRIVE THROUGH THE WINDOW. The green Ibiza parks in front of the studio and she watches him struggle out of the front seat. Vasil takes his arm and hands him a crutch. He leans on it, crosses the street, and heads straight for the shop.

"He tried to talk me out of it," he says, taking off his dark felt hat to reveal a shiny bald spot with a few dark patches. "But I wanted to meet you. Even if they did say it was going to rain today."

Dolores says hello and offers him a chair. He sits down slowly, lays the crutch to one side, and stretches out his left leg until it's straight. Vasil stands next to him, his long umbrella like a crutch itself, a cloth bag hanging from his arm.

"Do you need anything?" she asks.

"The chair is fine. Very kind of you."

Since she watched him get out of the car, she's understood why the woman called him *the old man*. It's not just his age—Clemente Artés has something not quite of this world. It's evident in his dress: the perfectly ironed shirt, the linen jacket, the black kerchief knotted around his neck. Even old people from here don't dress that way, especially not in summer. Nor do they have his long, carefully trimmed white beard, which looks like something from a nineteenth-century postcard. He reminds her of the photos of Charles Darwin she saw in the encyclopedia. Even without speaking, he seems like a foreigner. But then he does speak, hesitantly, as if struggling to pronounce the words, as if he'd forgotten them and had to translate them from French in his mind:

"More than forty years away from your country turn you into a foreigner," he admits with a smile after Dolores asks him how long he lived in France. "But in the end, home always comes calling. Don't you think?"

Dolores notices his perfect teeth, the wrinkles in his forehead, the deep furrows next to his eyes. When he smiles, his face turns friendly. The change is striking. How old must he be? Eighty-five? Maybe older. His bearing is formal. It could be the French education. No one here ever stands on ceremony. She thinks all this as she hands him the envelope.

He opens it quickly and delicately removes the photos from inside. Careful, touching the paper in a way that betrays years of experience with the materials.

"*Très belles*," he murmurs, almost to himself. Then, addressing Dolores, he says, "Very lovely."

She thinks they are anything but.

"I realize *lovely* is perhaps not the best word," he continues, as if he's read these thoughts on her face, "but to me, they are. As photos, but also because of what they represent." He's transfixed by one of them for a moment and adds, "It happens to us all, dear friend... there you are."

He looks through the rest of the photos, then takes one and asks Vasil to hand him the beige cloth bag he's brought along. Dolores remembers it from before, when Vasil came to pick up the first batch of copies, the Kodak logo yellow and red in the middle. The man removes a large album with a purple velvet cover and gilded metal corners, opening it and placing the picture into a small frame cut into one of its pages.

"I wanted to show this to you, for you to know how important what you've done for me is," he says, placing the album in front of Dolores.

She leans over and sees an image of the man she photographed, smiling.

"Life and death," he says. "I've got more friends in this album than out of it."

Dolores doesn't know what to say.

"Do you keep all your... friends here?"

"Just the ones I'm closest with. Don't think there are so many people who truly matter in the course of a life. With time, you start forgetting their faces. I remember everything else, but the faces start to blur." He looks at her closely. "Have you ever lost anyone?"

"Too many people," she responds without thinking.

"Then you know what I'm talking about."

Dolores nods. Clemente Artés is right, she thinks. But she will never forget Luis's face. She never could. It's there for her at every single moment, she could draw it with each detail intact if she knew how to handle a pencil. But which face? At which instant? What is the image of Luis she has in her head? The sum of all those she still has of him. Fleeting moments, imprecise. And the photos, of course. Especially the photos. Maybe. Because it's true that increasingly she remembers him through printed images rather than scenes she preserves in memory. And there's one moment in particular that's missing from the sequence. One she will never be able to return to. An emptiness that expands at times and saps the consistency from everything else.

"You may find this ridiculous," Clemente Artés continues, "but I need a reminder close to hand." He runs his fingers over the photo. "That includes their final moments. Today, death horrifies us, and we conceal it so it won't bother anyone, but as you must know, the dead were the very first photographic subjects. Bodies, objects, landscapes...you know, in French we call a still life *nature morte*, dead nature, of course in Spanish you do too. *Naturaleza muerta*. It's fitting. There is nothing macabre in preserving the image of a loved one no longer here. It's an act of devotion. I can't conceive of how we've abandoned that tradition."

Dolores grimaces but says nothing. It's always been hard for her to find words, and she's tended to rely on body language and gesture. She moves her lips to one side and furrows her forehead to show chagrin. Luis stole that look from her, she realized that one day when she saw him doing it. Now, whenever the skin of her face goes taut, she can't forget the history of that expression.

It turns noisy, and the three of them look outside. It's raining, hard.

Vasil picks up the umbrella.

"It's going to be bad," he says.

"They call it the weatherman's woe," Dolores says. She heard that on the radio today. It's also known as a cutoff low, and they used to call it a cold drop: a trough cut off from the westerly currents. "It's the season. I hope there's no flooding this time. This town's cursed."

"We'll go now, just in case." Clemente Artés puts the album into the cloth bag and rests it on his legs.

That is when the proposal comes. Without preambles. Less a proposal than a plea: to help him with his photographs of the dead. There aren't many such commissions. Just a token few.

"I don't want this to just end. It's important. But as you can see, I'm not much use anymore."

For a moment, Dolores doesn't know how to react.

"I don't know that I'm ready for something like that" is all she can think of to say.

"You have the eye...I wouldn't ask you if I hadn't noticed something special. Believe me, I've been doing this a long time."

"I appreciate the compliment, but..."

"Just think it over. You can't imagine how much these photographs mean for those who are mourning a loss. And they pay well. Much more than I gave you. People don't pinch pennies when it comes to death."

Before getting up, the old man looks back in the cloth bag and takes out a book that resembles an album.

"Here," he says, offering it to her. "It's a gift."

She thanks him and lays it on the counter.

"I wrote it years ago," he says. "Maybe it will show you how important these things are."

Dolores reads the title, stamped on the clothbound cover: *The Last Image*. Instinctively, she runs her fingers over the letters. The author is unnamed.

"Thanks a lot. I'll look at it closely."

"Let me know," he replies, getting out of his chair with Vasil's help.

Outside, it's raining even harder.

"Are you sure you don't want to wait for it to stop?"

"It doesn't look like it will. We picked the worst day to come."

"I bring car over," Vasil says, taking the bag, opening the door, and running out toward the Seat Ibiza as though taking flight.

Dolores gives the old man her arm and stands there with him till Vasil returns. His grip is strong. His body tense, heavy. He doesn't smell like an old man. His aroma reminds her of newly chopped wood, a carpenter's shop, but also damp earth.

She walks him a few feet to the car while Vasil holds the umbrella over them. She opens the door and eases him in.

"See? I need you." He smiles as he tumbles into the seat.

Dolores smiles back.

"Take care," she says, and hurries back into the shop. Just thirty seconds she's been out there, but it's as if someone's drenched her with buckets of water. Her blouse is clinging to her body, and even her bra is soaked.

She watches through the window as the car vanishes in the rain. Then she pulls her hair back from her forehead and wipes off her face. The old man's aroma is still on her hands.

7

THE FIRST THING SHE DOES AFTER WATCHING
the news is call her son. Come home, Iván, she wants to
say. Come before it gets worse, and stay with me through
the storm. But instead, after apologizing for interrupting
his routine in the city, she tells him the contrary:

"Don't even think about getting on the road
tomorrow."

It's Thursday, and school's just started. Iván is supposed to spend the weekend at home. But she wants him
to stay in Murcia. Even if the news there is worrisome too.
Better there than on the roads. She'll have to be alone. But
anyway, she always is. He could come see her every week.
Every day, if he wanted. It's just forty minutes from the
capital to the village. But he'd always been determined to
live close to school. It was better for his studies. Commu-
nications and media. What he really wanted to study was
film. At least he didn't go to Madrid.

He's better off there, she thinks to herself, far from
the sorrow, the melancholy of home. But today she

wishes he was close to her. So she could protect him from the storm. Even being with him in the city would be better. To not feel the difference, short as it may be. Distance always means possibly not getting there in time. Being late. When there's nothing more you can do.

"Don't worry, Mom, I won't leave. I've got stuff to do this weekend."

This eases her mind, but in her heart, she wishes he'd argue with her, not yield to common sense. What do you mean, don't come, Mom, how could I leave you there and stay here just because I have *stuff to do?* How could I not catch the bus, or drive, or even walk under the rain to make it home so the two of us could hold each other and keep each other warm? How could I not drop everything, Mom, to be with you as the sky rips open and everything collapses? No, Iván just says, don't worry, he'll be fine, as if nothing were happening, as if he felt free of the obligation to have to return to a home marred by afflictions.

After dinner, Dolores peeks out the window. It's still raining hard. Lightning gleams on the stream where the street once stood. Soon after comes the thunder, its roar encircling the house.

She remembers all at once what happened three years ago, in December of 2016. No one could forget. The rain, the flooded ravines, the swamped streets. She'd seen something like that as a teenager too. The town was cursed, she'd told Clemente Artés that afternoon. But it's also fated to resist, to rise up over and again, not caring that the world was going to hell. Every time the rain comes, though, the disquiet and uncertainty return. The fear. The resignation.

Hopefully this time it will blow over.

She unplugs the TV. Unscrews the coaxial cable. She's never known why she does this, but her mother used to do it too. Or unhook the antenna, rather. The antenna attracts lightning, she used to say. The TV does, all electronic appliances do. It also hits the plumbing and it can come out if you open the tap. One neighbor had to have his finger amputated, another had lightning come right through his window. So you close everything and keep quiet, play hide-and-go-seek. This is just superstition, she thinks, but she can't help it, it's part of the ritual when the storm comes. Like checking the batteries in the flashlight and getting the candles and lighter ready in case the power turns off.

Tonight, though, the lights have held out. Still, she keeps the angular flashlight on her nightstand, with a candle stuffed in an empty beer bottle next to a lighter. She picks up the book Clemente Artés gave her. It's not the best reading for a stormy night. But it's piqued her curiosity.

When she opens it, the old man's aroma returns. And she smells something else this time, not just cut wood, but a vinegary scent that reminds her of fixer in a tray. She's sure of it: that scent impregnates the entire book. She finds a large whitish spot on the cloth binding. And more than one wrinkled page. As if he'd spilled fixer on the book itself. She strokes the cloth and turns the wavy pages. Then, instinctively, she brings them to her lips. The book smells like photography, and it tastes like it too.

Perhaps for that reason, everything she reads that night takes on a special bodily reality, even the dedication, which confronts her as soon as she's begun leafing through it: *To Gisèle, in life and in death.*

She doesn't intend to read it now, but she can't help glancing at the index and introduction, along with a few of the photographs. Right away, she realizes Clemente Artés isn't an essayist, exactly. The book is a kind of inventory, tallying works, compositional techniques, iconographical information. There is a ten-page introduction and several paragraphs before each selection of images. The illustrations vastly exceed the amount of text.

Like every photography aficionado, Dolores knows of the tradition of mortuary photography. It's mentioned in the histories of photography she has at home. It's an old practice, one that has always put her in mind of nineteenth-century eccentricity, a strange custom from the beginnings of the art, one of many pathways that receded and vanished in time.

In his introduction, Clemente Artés delves into the origins of postmortem photography, the *last image*, as he apparently prefers to call it. The tradition of representing the dead predates photography and lies in the very origins of art itself. "The mystery of life and death," he writes, "the beginning of representation." Artés alludes to Pliny the Elder's fable about the origin of art: the Maid of Corinth traces on a rock the silhouette of her beloved before he embarks on a long journey. "The image as a form of mourning, as the memory of an absence."

Mortuary photography is the drawing into the present of the last image—an attempt to capture what is on the verge of being erased. It is linked to the spread of photography in the modern era. "Everyone had to have a photo. Not to have one meant not to have existed. Not to have one was to run the risk of not being remembered." Throughout, Artés is prone to these episodes of would-be lyricism in his attempts to pin down the meaning of his subject. "To capture the figure," "to entrap the memory," "to pin the body down before it vanishes forever."

She'll go back to the text later, she tells herself. Right now, she's more tempted by the photographs. The book catalogues them in three broad categories: the living, the sleeping, and the dead. These categories suggest a peculiar attitude toward death, denial, and acceptance.

As she turns the pages, she finds dead people who appear to be asleep. Others with eyes open, so it's hard to distinguish them from the living. She pays special attention to the children, held by their mothers or posed in the company of their siblings, all of whom stare straight into the camera. The eyes of the dead are wide-open. Those photos are the most unsettling, at least to her. Much more so than those in which the dead are posed as if asleep. In bed, on a divan, in an armchair: the corpse with eyes closed, in a state of lethargy or "eternal sleep," as the book has it. Really, it's hard for her to grasp that they are truly dead and not simply at rest.

Finally, there are the deceased portrayed as such, as lifeless bodies. Death is natural here, mundane. The coffin. Flowers. The wake and the burial. The body in repose, the body in the company of friends and family. Again, the contrast: some of the living look far more dead than the dead themselves.

As she contemplates them, she feels something pulling her in and repelling her at once. It's not just the sordidness of it, though she knows that must be what most people find alluring here. It's something that goes beyond curiosity. A feeling that starts in her chest and extends through her body. Sorrow. That's the word. Grief, expanding at the sight of these children, faces sleepy, serene, mouths open slightly, fingers interlaced, little hands... More than once, she has to stop to take a breath.

She's certain she shouldn't see this, and it unsettles her to do so: these images that once were private, treasured memories intended for loved ones. To see them is to enter, almost to profane, a world of others. The feeling grows more intense as the photos become more recent, some of them taken in the eighties, in color, bringing everything into the present. It's strange to her that this tradition continued so late into the twentieth century, so close to her own time.

She can't help but notice the credits of the photos are all the same: the Artés Blanco Collection. She hasn't counted, but there must be a hundred fifty of them, of diverse techniques (daguerreotype, albumin, collodion, gelatin) and origins: the majority French, but others English, American, Spanish.

She'd like to see the originals one day. Even if, as the pages turn, her dejection and listlessness have worsened. Along with a burdened feeling in her temples.

The discomfort is worst when she reaches the last page. In black and white, centered, without a caption, is the reproduction of a daguerreotype. Or so she thinks, though there's no reference to the technique, the photographer, or the collection it belongs to. It's a colophon, and it seems not to belong to the sequence that precedes it. Something in it makes her turn her head away. Something that disturbs her, though she can't say what. All the elements are perfectly defined, almost saturated: the frieze of wallpaper in what might be a bedroom, the curtain in the back, the landscape over the bedstead, the glass of water on the nightstand. Everything except the figure of the deceased—or what she imagines must be the deceased, a man or a woman, a white shadow on the bed—whose body is blurry, veiled in haze. She can see, just barely, a spot over what must be the face.

The contrast between the limpid surroundings and the vagueness of the body in the bed turns her stomach, sends a bitter aftertaste up into her throat. Too many dead for one person's eyes to see, she thinks, closing the book and leaving it on the nightstand. Probably it's the storm, the unceasing thunder, the penetrating scent of fixer that's gotten to her. That odor hovers all night around the bed. And the images don't go away when she turns off the light and gets under the sheets, despite the heat. Everything is still there, and closing her eyes doesn't help. Above all, that vaporous gray impressed on her retina, lingering like a fog that refuses to lift.

At least I don't believe in ghosts, she thinks. Otherwise, she might feel that the photo was possessing her. This crosses her mind as she tries to sleep and the dense absence by her side steals her breath. She refuses to open her eyes and look at it. She knows it's darker than darkness itself.

II

A MIRROR WITH MEMORY

· · ·

1

WHEN HE CROUCHES IS WHEN HE REMINDS HER most of Luis. She can't help looking at him from the corner of her eye, pants rolled to his knees, boots covered in mud, trying to clear the sludge from the living room of the beach house. He offered to help. If it had been up to her, he'd still be in the capital. But deep down, she's happy he ignored the recommendations of the police last night and found a way to come home.

Her renters have helped too. Fortunately, only about five inches of water came in. They listened to the Civil Guard and raised up everything they could. But she'll probably have to buy new furniture for next year. Sofas and dressers. A dining room table. The parts made of particleboard have already started to swell.

The house had been rented till the end of September, but summer here is over for now. The people told her this morning: when they're done cleaning, they'll go back to Madrid. She doesn't need to worry about the money: they'll pay the whole sum, as they agreed to months ago, and as they've done since they started renting the house seven years ago. Loyalty, Dolores thinks. But she's also never bumped up the price. And she holds it for them every year. She hopes they'll come back next summer.

Cleaning and thinking about what happened just two streets farther up, she realizes she's been lucky. There are houses and shops where the water rose two feet. They'll have to throw out everything. She just needs to buy a bit of furniture, paint the walls, not much else. Yes, she was lucky. Here, in the house she rents out, and in the one she lives in too. There, just a little water got into the garage. Luis always used to say: *This house is an island.*

This is what occurs to her as she helps Iván shovel dirt into the basket. They've never had to clean up so much. The more they take out, the more appears. It never ends. Only days later do the tiles of the floor begin to recover their old color. The brown on the grout, she thinks, will probably never go away. Like the scent of damp and rot and muck, the invisible memory of the flood.

At home, she prefers not to watch the news. She's had those images in her head for days: the flooded village, the little sea merging with the violent ochre water of the ravines, the waterlogged houses, the destroyed shops, the powerless faces of neighbors, the tears, the complaints, the anguish. She needs to think of something else—talk about something else. Perhaps that's why she tells Iván about Clemente Artés: the phone call, the visit, the photos, the book.

She mentions him, too, because it's the only topic of conversation that allows her not to be a mother treating her son like a boy without a father. When they talk about photography, it's as if she were talking to Luis, as if her husband, what remains of him in the body of his twenty-two-year-old son, had suddenly appeared. True, they don't look much alike: everyone says, with his round face and curly hair, he takes after her. But he does have some of his father's gestures: the way his hands flap frantically as he talks, like an orchestra conductor's, and the way he blinks and opens his eyes wide when something excites or interests him. There are times when it hurts to look at him.

He was a papa's boy. Longed for. Come too late. She was almost forty, and he was well past it. They'd tried everything. All the different treatments, at least the ones they could afford. Then, when they'd practically lost hope, she got pregnant. Dolores thinks she can even remember the night he was conceived. The next day, she got up feeling her body transformed.

From the first, it unsettled her that her child's parents would be as old as grandparents. She'd known couples like that. Her cousin Amelia—she'd been a mistake, she used to say, had almost immediately had to start

49

taking care of her parents, and was frustrated that she'd never known them when they were young. What Dolores couldn't imagine was that Iván wouldn't see his father turn into a grandfather, that he would remember him young—or as young as you can be at fifty-four—forever.

She did her best. But she couldn't avoid difficulties. That's to be expected, she's often thought. Your world falls apart and you realize nothing makes sense. If it didn't for her, and she'd lived half her life almost, how could it for an eleven-year-old boy?

The first months were hardest. Iván barely spoke, was angry at the world, as if what had happened to his father were everyone's fault. Dolores felt that same resentment, but she had to pretend she was fine and everything was in order. She had to keep taking care of the family. Her young son and her father, who needed her for almost everything.

One afternoon, Iván found an envelope with some of Luis's photos she had developed. Dolores didn't have to tell him what it meant to bring his way of seeing things back into the present. The next day, he asked her for one of Luis's cameras and a few cartridges of color and black-and-white film. He'd lived surrounded by photographs, but technique had never interested him. For months, he barely put the camera down. He photographed his father's negatives, his cameras, his equipment, his clothes, the corners of the house that reminded him of him, drawing an unconscious map of his remembrance.

Dolores developed the photos with a timid heart. Every one of them was like a knife. But she did it for her son. Despite the pain, there was something curative in it. At least for Iván. The photos allowed him to accept the loss, if not get past it, in a way she never managed to understand.

Maybe it was his age, kids adapt to change better than adults, or maybe it was something else, but Iván managed to move on while she remained there, stranded in time. Sometimes she imagines a road with two people walking on it, and slowly, one loses sight of the other. The feeling is ambiguous. She's glad to see him turn the page, but at the same time, she can't avoid the feeling that Iván has left her alone with her grief, that grief she tried to save him from and that she now has all to herself. It's hard for her to admit it, but there are times when she wants everyone else to join her in mourning. All of them. Iván, Teresa too. For them to come back to the pain and sorrow, be immobilized by that dark absence, sink with her in the dim swamp she's still never found a way out of.

She tries to conceal these thoughts, stuffing them deep inside. But sometimes they come out, and she doesn't know how to stop them.

"You don't respect anything. Is this any way to show love for your father?" she shouted at Iván early one morning after Halloween when he came home hungover to accompany her to the cemetery, with the stamp from a nightclub still on the back of his hand.

Maybe that's why he distances himself. She can see it on his face, in his silences, in that enclosed solitude that she interprets as a rejection of her endless bereavement. And she knows that, too, is why for four years, Iván's only ever come home on the occasional weekend.

"Between my internship and work, I can't get a minute free," he often says by way of an excuse.

"This isn't a movie from America," she replies. "We have a family here. You have a home. You have a mother, alone... You must miss her, right?"

"Don't blackmail me, Mom," is his inevitable response.

And it upsets her because she knows she's doing it. At least in part. Emotional blackmail. She tries to avoid it, but over and over she finds herself resorting to it. What can she do? He's her son, and she'd like to have him with her at all times. And yet, she tries to understand him and sometimes she even does. He wants to be in the city, not in the village. Going home for him means returning to the past. It's like they live in different eras, as if mother and son were divided by an unbreachable distance, the untranscribable measures of grief's cycles.

Only photography breaches the distance, the world rebuilding itself in those moments, images making a common language possible. This is happening tonight, as Dolores talks about the photos and shows her son the book Clemente Artés gave her.

"It looks like the book from *The Others*," Iván says, "that Amenábar movie with Nicole Kidman."

"I know it." She saw it at the theater with Luis when Iván was just three or four years old.

"This is wild! And you're going to get involved with this?"

"I still don't know."

Dolores shows him the proofs of her own photos from the funeral home, and her son looks at them, rapt.

"The shadows and reflections were hard to deal with. The gleam of the coffin overwhelmed everything else."

"What camera did you take?"

"Your dad's F4. With Tri-X 400 that expired four years ago."

"For real? You just risked it? What did you do to keep it from fogging?"

"It's magic, Son. And a touch of overexposure. But on the positives, you can hardly see it. There's a bit more grain, but nothing you'd really notice."

As she talks, Dolores sees Iván staring at her with satisfaction in his eyes. Or at least with normalcy. It's photography, of course, that does that to him, same as always, but it's her, too, she feels more alive today, as if those photos, for reasons she doesn't quite understand, were rescuing her from her lethargy.

"Call him, Mom," he finally suggests. "Other people's deaths do you good."

2

THE SIGHT OF THE TWO OF THEM WALKING through the door of the funeral home is like something from a film noir. Or so Dolores thinks, imagining the scene from without: the old man, tall and thin, with his black hat and dark-gray suit, leaning on a wooden cane with a silver pommel, and her beside him, robust, in dark clothing, with the folded tripod and the brown leather backpack on her back with the photographic equipment inside.

They're walking slowly. She can tell he's tired. Clemente Artés seems to have gotten better over the past few days. But it's an illusion. He said so this morning when she picked him up at home.

"I'm walking better," he told her, "but I'm not the same man as before."

Panting, he thanked her for accepting on such short notice. He called last night without warning and proposed she accompany him to the funeral home the next day. Without her help, he'd have to turn down the commission.

Dolores didn't have to think about it too long. It had been so often on her mind over the foregoing weeks that she was almost waiting for the call.

"You can't renounce your gift," he said before hanging up.

With those words in her head, she went to bed last night and then got up at dawn. She put on her black cotton pants and an ash-gray blouse and had her coffee standing in the kitchen before putting the old man's address in her phone. Even with GPS, it was hard to find in that half-built development of bare walls, empty lots...She thought she was in the wrong place until she found his street.

"It's a wasteland here," he told her as they were driving away. "I thought I was moving to heaven and I didn't even make it out of limbo."

In the thirty minutes it took to reach the funeral home, Clemente has explained the job to her. It's a young woman. Forty. Cancer. Dead in less than a year. He told her with his eyes on the road, showing hardly any emotion.

"Why would someone want to memorialize a disfigured body?" Dolores couldn't help but ask. "With all the photos you take of people when they're alive..."

"Because that body is still your wife, your mother, your daughter...until the end. In sickness. Even in death. And it's not just the body they want to remember, they want to remember the moment. Even the coffin they hold on to. The last embrace before closing the lid, the last time they can see the person they love. *Et c'est tout.*"

The widower receives them in the vestibule, a big, polite man with a beard and a hat. Unlike the daughter of Clemente's friend, who showed her discomfort when Dolores arrived at the funeral home with her camera and tripod, the young husband makes everything easy for them. After all, he was the one who asked for the photo. Dolores still doesn't get it.

Many hesitate when the funeral home offers this service, Clemente told her in the car. Most of them say no. But those who do agree accept it immediately, as something natural, somehow grasping its deeper significance. And that's why they try to make it easy on them, because they know something important is going to happen.

The old man gingerly gives his hand to the man with the beard.

"I'm very sorry," he says. "I hope this photo helps you."

She observes his behavior, his manners, his ritual. His approach is like that of the funeral home employees, intimate but distant, just affectionate enough to distract from the management's indifference.

She remembers what he told her on the way: coolness helps. The pain is theirs. You can't take it away from them. With time, you come to understand that.

A funeral home employee accompanies them to the chapel, where they find the family members sitting in chairs and eyeing them suspiciously, apparently with no idea what's going on. Someone approaches the young widower and whispers in his ear. He responds inaudibly and takes the man's hands, trying to calm him. Dolores senses the family may have argued about the photo. The man looks at them and says it's fine, they can carry on with their work. They approach the large glass panel that looks onto the woman in the coffin, surrounded by bouquets of flowers and wreaths. As the employee inserts the key in the door to the little chamber, the husband pauses briefly, perhaps from a sudden change of heart. Clemente looks at him in silence. She tries to do the same.

Once inside, Dolores feels the cold on her cheeks. This time, her arms are covered, she's had the foresight to bring a black leather jacket.

"You can stay if you like," Clemente tells the widower.

He spoke about this in the car on the way over, when she asked if the families often entered the cold chamber despite its narrow dimensions. It's the best way for them to feel no one's taking anything from them, he said. They want to be with their loved ones the whole time. It comforts them not to leave as we take the photos. And they remember the moment better. Lets them start to say goodbye.

When it's time to take the pictures, Clemente hardly speaks. Like a surgeon, he asks for lenses, tripod, to move a small reflector to soften the shadows. He asks, he never tells her this or that is how it must be done.

Dolores avoids looking at the deceased. Her eyes wander from place to place, trying not to settle on anything except Clemente's face. Before the process begins, he stands still for a few seconds in front of the body. You have to see the photo in your mind before you peer through the lens. She knows. Your eyes take the photo first, only then does the camera.

Dolores studies his movements, the ritual of respect, notices his stillness, as if time had frozen in the cold. There aren't so many photos to take, and technically, it's not hard. Arrange the tripod, which they use even for the detailed shots of the face, the hands, the flowers. Frame, focus, adjust the depth of field, leave the shutter open for a longer exposure... At each step, Clemente is deliberate, attentive. This, too, he spoke of in the car:

"The body doesn't move, *c'est vrai*. But we're not just capturing the body, we're capturing the air, the substances that are there but can't be seen."

Dolores has always known there was a ceremonial aspect to this work. But that was abstract to her until she saw Clemente motionless behind the lens. And she can't help thinking of Luis. Of how her husband would have interpreted the scene. For him, too, photography captured things not visible to the eye. The atmosphere, the intangible. He used to say what you didn't see was what mattered. Dolores always thought this was dewy-eyed mysticism. More than once, they argued about it. She believed—she still does—that photography makes things more visible, distances them from their surroundings so they can better be seen. She's never acknowledged there could be something else there that the photo was supposed to capture. By definition, the invisible can't be seen. Let alone portrayed.

But she doesn't argue with Clemente. She just observes him. In his eyes, she sees something she never saw in Luis. Luis's eyes betrayed intuition, Clemente's show certainty, faith. He seems to have sensed what she's thinking:

"This is much more than a photograph. It's an act of memory. An homage."

When they leave, she feels as though she's returned to the real world once more. The sun is high in the sky. She takes off her leather jacket. A warm breeze caresses her arms. It's October now, but the cold still hasn't come.

On the way home, they barely discuss what they've done. Clemente seems to need the silence. He's tired, she can tell.

"It's important," he says finally. "Respect. I think you see it that way too."

Dolores nods. There's no need for words now.

She drives to his house and walks him to the door. Vasil receives them and helps with the equipment.

Dolores peeks into the hall, just managing to see all the photos hanging on the walls. It's like a gallery.

"Do you want to stay for lunch?" Clemente asks.

"Another day. When there's more time."

She knows the day will come. And the time will come with it.

3

SHE DEVELOPS THE FILM IN HER STUDIO. CLE-
mente said she could take it to the lab he normally uses,
but Dolores said she'd rather do it herself. She feels closer
to the deceased woman emerging on the paper than she
did in the funeral home. She notices the contrast between her face and the flowers in the background. The
profile sharp, the flowers blurred. Hard as it is to admit,
she finds a certain beauty in the image. Beyond the
tragedy it discloses. Maybe because it's black and white,
which makes it feel less immediate. Clemente said that
on the phone: color is too specific, too obvious. Even if
it's just a convention, black and white opens time, showing not a concrete moment in history, but an abstraction
of the past, of memory.

The woman's haggard face, consumed by disease,
belongs not just to the definite instant of the day of her
death. The black-and-white aura detemporizes it. Especially for those who knew that face when it was young
and healthy.

The body she observes will be different from the one the young widower will see. She is contemplating the last image of a face seen in isolation. For the woman's husband and all those who knew her, though, it will be a fragment in a series, the face in one state, in one moment. They will compare it with expressions they knew before. They'll say: How the illness ate away at her, and she was such a beauty. They'll say: She doesn't look like the woman she was. Or they'll say: They've captured her essence. No matter how much she suffered, it's her face. Her body. It's still her. Even there. Wife, sister, daughter, aunt, friend. Because there, in that face suspended in time, all those other faces are contained. Life and death, intertwined.

How can a face cease to be a face, how can death turn a familiar surface into a foreign expanse? With Luis, she never found out. His face is out of field. An empty image. With her father, it happened in just a few seconds, after his last breath, and it remains imprinted on her retina. As it does with her mother and all those known and loved ones she's looked at through the window in the funeral home. And yet, for some reason, the one that still stands out is the face in death of her grandmother Remedios.

Nana Reme. It's better you remember her as she was in life, her aunt told her the day she died. Dolores was nine years old, and Nana hadn't yet turned eighty. She's thought about that many times afterward. For her, Nana

Reme was always an old woman in mourning, the pockets of her apron full of handkerchiefs and papers.

She became bedbound not long after Dolores started school, and held out that way for three and a half years. Without complaints. I'm fine, she always said on those nights when Dolores would go kiss her good night and she'd smile and hold her hand a few seconds. Even on the night she died. Get some rest, Lolica, she said, as if that night were no different from any other, clutching her hand tight, with the same smile as always.

From her bedroom, Dolores heard the commotion. She got up and found the door closed. She waited outside until her mother emerged. Nana's dead, she said, eyes red, face damp. Go back to your room. No theatrics, just an order: Stay in your room, don't get in the way. She can't forget that silence, as though everything had stopped. And then the sudden agitation. In the middle of the night. In a matter of seconds.

With the door cracked, she watched people coming in and out of the room. The neighbors. The doctor. And finally, the people from the funeral home. She only figured that out later, thinking about what happened that night. In the moment, all she saw was people. People in the room, people in the house, gathering, more and more. And chairs. Endless chairs. She can't get that out of her head. The neighbor ladies brought lots of them, but most came from the bar, brought over by her father. Metal chairs in the hallway.

She also remembers the scent of coffee. Her aunt Josefa making pots of coffee. She was the one who took care of her that night, who tried to make her a part of it. Come on, Lolica, help me with the glasses. She tried to explain to her what was happening:

"You know your nana died, right? She went out like a candle. She didn't suffer. She's gone to a better place. She's in heaven, with Big Juan"—that's what they called her grandfather—"and she's resting. We'll have to pray for her, but don't worry, don't get upset."

Dolores hasn't forgotten that conversation. Her aunt talked to her about death like she was a little girl. She nodded along, but she didn't believe that story about Nana being in heaven. She was in her room. And Dolores wanted to see her. More than anything in the world.

"Don't go in there, Lolica," her aunt said. "It's best if you remember her as she was."

That was the phrase: Remember her as she was. But how was she? Her expression hadn't changed much since the night before when she kissed her and told her good night. She was her nana Reme. She had died, how could Dolores not go in there, how could what she saw in there spoil her memory of her? And so she ignored the warnings and burst in. And what she saw there remained with her forever.

Nana was in a big wooden coffin, raised up on two small metal supports. The first thing Dolores thought was they must have had to look for an extra-large coffin to fit her tubby body, two-hundred-twenty-plus pounds, as her mother always said. A white satin cloth covered her, leaving only her head exposed. Dolores wondered if she had on a nightgown or one of her black dresses underneath, or the apron with dark stripes she used to always wear. She looked over at the coat stand to see if it was hanging there, unknotted, pockets full of handkerchiefs.

What captured her attention immediately was her face. She wondered if her aunt was right. That face, it wasn't exactly Nana's. Something had changed. The skin was matte yellow, like wax. And she was serious, lips pursed, looking glued together—which they were, though she didn't know that then. Her smile, the one she had said good night with a few hours before dying, was gone. Those were her features, but that wasn't her face.

Dolores was paralyzed for a few moments in front of the coffin. She didn't come closer, didn't touch her, didn't kiss her. She didn't cry either. She couldn't yet grasp that her nana wouldn't come back, that she was dead and had left them. What she was seeing muffled any and all feelings. It was an image she still didn't know how to interpret.

Her mother wouldn't stop crying, and Dolores couldn't comfort her. As far back as she can remember, she had always tried. But in that moment, she was cold in a way she now thinks was unsuited to a nine-year-old girl. Later she did cry disconsolately. The tears burst forth when the coffin left through the front door. It was then that she realized Nana really was somewhere else, that she was leaving what had been her home. And she asked herself why they had to take her away so soon, why they couldn't just leave her a while longer.

She hasn't forgotten the days afterward. The darkness. The silence. The house became a kind of cave. The rolling blinds down, the TV turned off. Her mother's black dresses, dark leggings, and unwashed hair. She aged suddenly, withering overnight.

The bar didn't open for three days. That was the only time she ever missed the noise. Her mother went back to work a week later.

The TV was kept on in the bar. At first the voices there seemed muted, but the dinging of the slot machine and the clamor of the Sunday soccer games enlivened the place. When she got home, the silence and darkness returned. That was the only time in her life she ever preferred being at the bar.

She doesn't know how long her mother took to turn on the TV in the living room again. Weeks. Weeks, too, to roll the blinds back up and take off her mourning clothes. What she does know is she didn't enter Nana's bedroom for more than a year. And the image of the body in the coffin is still with her.

She's lost her parents, her dearest friends, the love of her life. But the clearest image of death remains the one from that night: that figure, that silence, that sorrow she still can't understand. There are images that accompany us forever and, like an invisible mold, shape all that comes after them. She understands this today, developing a photo of a stranger's inert face and feeling a sharp splinter pierce her memory.

4

THIS TIME, THE HOUSE IS EASIER TO FIND, AT
the outer edge of the half-finished development. She
looks at the construction company's billboards, faded,
almost white, and is unsurprised to see the name of
Teresa's ex-husband's employer, Futura Maris. She always thought that sounded pretentious, and more like
something from the past than of the future. But as she
contemplates the ruins of the unfinished houses, she
thinks to herself that it was apt. This may have been
the last development before the bubble burst and they
stopped being able to pay their creditors. Apart from
a few streets, which must be from phase one, the entire place is a pile of relics. Corroding machines, rotting materials, fossilized into the terrain. Everything
looks abandoned overnight, as if, when the good times
ended, people had left in a stampede, not even returning to retrieve the scaffolds or bring down the cranes,
now stranded forever in a future that never became
present.

This is what she feels as she passes over the streets, the strange sensation of coming both before and after. And the awareness of desolation, of dejection, at something extinguished before it ever began.

She parks and takes the proofs of the photos she's developed out of the back seat. She glances at the clock on the dashboard: a quarter to twelve. She rolled down the blinds at the shop today almost as soon as she'd rolled them up.

Clemente opens the door and invites her in. Even at home, he dresses elegantly. Dolores notices the shine on his dark leather shoes. She's never gotten hers to gleam like that, no matter how hard she's tried.

He's alone, he tells her. Vasil's off that day. She doesn't say anything, but thinks that a man of his age and in his condition should have someone with him.

Leaning on his cane, he guides her to the living room. His aroma, that scent of recently cut wood, extends through every corner of the house.

She tries to avoid looking curious as she notices every detail around her, especially the photos on the wall, and the cameras, the lenses, the reflectors, the light meters on the shelves.

"You've got quite a museum here," she says as she settles into the large leather sofa that dominates the room.

"I like having all this around me. I've got nothing else left."

Before sitting next to her, he rolls over a bar cart from beside the bookshelf and asks, "Would you care for a drink? A pastis?"

Dolores nods. She likes the long, soft esses in his speech.

Slowly, he lifts a bottle of Ricard and places it on the small coffee table in front of the sofa. He helps himself along, leaning on the furnishings, as he walks toward what must be the kitchen and returns with a bottle of water and glasses filled with ice on a tray.

Dolores instinctively gets up to help him, but Clemente tells her not to worry. He reaches the table, sits down, and slowly mixes the liquor with water.

"You have to dilute it or the anise taste is too strong."

The bottle looks familiar, maybe she's seen it somewhere in a bar, but she's never tried it. She does notice the anise taste, but it's soft and refreshing.

"It's one of those French habits I just can't escape. Of course, I don't allow myself much."

Dolores takes out the photos and puts them on the table. Clemente examines them one by one.

"We did a good job, don't you think?"

She nods and takes a sip. The ice is starting to melt and the beverage tastes less sweet than before.

"I like the contrast of the face and flowers," she says. "The black and white makes it all less concrete. You were right. But your book has some color photos in it."

"Not many. Color is violent. It exerts too great an effect on the moment. That's why I've always preferred black and white. At least for mortuary photos. It has an aura that comforts those who look at it."

He takes a sip and adds, "So you like the book?"

Like is probably not the word, she thinks. But she nods.

"It's your collection, right? Artés…"

"Artés Blanco," he corrects her. "Even by fate I was predisposed against color," he jokes, referring to his last name, *Blanco*. They laugh. "Would you like to see some of it?"

"If it's not a bother?"

Clemente struggles to his feet and motions for her to accompany him. She leaves her glass on the table, she's had enough, and follows him a few feet down the hallway. If the house reminds her of a gallery, the room they now enter is like a cabinet of curiosities.

"*This* is my private museum," he says when he opens the door. "Just for me. And now for you."

It's almost as big as the living room—it looks like two joined rooms—and is lined by dark wooden bookshelves and glass cabinets full of framed photos.

She needs time before she begins to recognize everything. They're the illustrations of the book, the entire collection unfolded before her. She remembers the classifications: the living, the sleeping, and the dead. The

71

photos in the vitrines follow the same order. With all the images there at once, a grand mortuary mosaic, the impression is more disturbing than in the book.

Clemente sits down, or rather, lets himself fall into a high-backed chair in the center of the room.

"I spend hours here sometimes, talking with these photographs in my mind."

He tells her he's been buying them for years. At antique shops and from individuals. He's catalogued all of them. In his own way. He has nearly two thousand of them. Only a small fraction made it into the book. He started collecting in Marseille, where he first discovered postmortem photography, and he still buys something now and again. The internet's made it all easier.

"A collection is never done," he admits. "Every photo is a testament to the end. When I sit here, I try to accept it. Accept that it will come for me. As it has come for all these you see here. It's important to be aware of that."

Dolores imagines him sitting in front of the photos, looking at them the way you look at an aquarium or a cinema screen. Or the way you pray in a mausoleum. The faint light, probably intended to keep from damaging the photos, and the dark tones of the carpet covering the floor reenforce that feeling of funereal intimacy. For a moment, it's as if she's in a cemetery. All that's missing is the scent of flowers.

She's seen many of these photos in the book, but their materiality startles her when she comes close to the vitrine. On the printed page, everything is uniform, but here the sizes, the frames, the grain, the texture of the paper, even the blacks and whites, are different. The photos here are not just images, but objects. Physical objects, occupying space.

This is especially true when she looks at the daguerreotypes. She had imagined them bigger. In their little wooden boxes, many are like tiny relics.

"You can open the cabinet and take them out," Clemente says. "That's how they mounted them, in fittings, like a watch. They're hard to find now. Postmortem daguerreotypes, I mean. And I can't pay such prices. But they're the crown jewels of the collection."

He repeats that they represent the true origins of photography. And the inner essence of mortuary photography. They are truly the last image. A paper photograph can be reproduced. But a daguerreotype is unique, like a painting.

"A mirror with memory," he concludes. "Literally. A moment in time that will never return. That is real death, the final reflection of a person's body."

Dolores opens the cabinet and takes one out carefully. She'd seen them from a distance in the photography class she took with Luis, but she's never held one in her hands. The wooden box that protects it is what she finds most striking. It's like a little book. Or a jewel case. She closes and opens it to see the image appear. She has to bend over, so the light won't reflect on it, to see. It's not easy to find the right angle. If she turns it too much to the side, the outline vanishes, and then it flips, and looks like a negative. Seeing it properly, she understands, is a precision maneuver, a discipline of the body.

She recognizes the figure she first saw in the book. It's one of the sleeping portraits. The girl is lying on a small divan, in deep slumber, hands folded, her bare feet emerging small from beneath a white dress. Dolores has to turn it slightly to see it. She's surprised by the figure's clear outlines, the exactness of its definition. Next to it, on the other side of the wooden case, is what seems to be a lock of hair held by a red ribbon and covered, like the daguerreotype itself, by a fine pane of glass.

"Is this..." she begins.

"Yes. What's left of the body. A vestige. Kept there like a jewel. A treasure. Which is exactly what it is."

"It's sad," she says, unable to take her eyes off the daguerreotype, to stop turning it, marveling at it like an amulet.

"And beautiful," he adds. "You have a human body in your hands."

Clemente's words are still reverberating in her head as they return to the living room, where Dolores notices a picture she had overlooked before. The reflections lead her to think it, too, is a daguerreotype, but it's bigger than the ones she was examining, and it's not in a box, but hanging on a wall in a frame. She has to stand aside and bend her neck to see it clearly. It's a woman's face, turned toward a window through which light is pouring in, holding a small child in her arms. It seems to have emerged from another time.

"My wife, Gisèle," Clemente interrupts her. "And my son, Eric."

"She's beautiful."

"She was. We came here to grow old together next to the sea, but she barely had the chance to enjoy it."

"I'm sorry. What about your son?"

"He's in Marseille. His life is there."

"When did you last see him?"

"His life is there," Clemente repeats bitterly, as if he didn't want to go further down that road. Or this is how it strikes Dolores, who decides it's time to leave. It's lunchtime, and she asks if he has anything ready. She doesn't know how to bring it up without sounding impertinent.

"Are you all alone here today?" is the only thing that occurs to her.

"Vasil's coming back at two," he says, easing her mind. "He'll bring a roast chicken from the village. Don't worry, I won't go hungry."

His response is blunt, ironic, but with a warning for her, a demarcation of boundaries: This is my life, everything's under control, and I don't need you coming and telling me what to do.

Before walking to the door and taking her hand to say goodbye, he says:

"Incidentally, it would be best if you delivered the photos yourself."

"Excuse me?"

"The photos we took. The widower needs them brought to him. Same as the flowers. It's a kind of homecoming. You'll knock on his door, but it isn't just you there. It's what you'll bring him. The restoration of something important."

5

"WHAT STRUCK ME MOST WAS HIS STARE," SHE confessed to her sister-in-law after ordering a bottle of Casa Castillo from the waiter. "How he stood there looking at the photo. The tenderness on his face. As if he were actually seeing his wife there."

"What did you say to him?"

"What could I say?"

She asked herself that same question this afternoon, and she still doesn't know how to respond. She should come up with an answer. Clemente wouldn't have had to think twice. She, once again, is dumbstruck.

She can't get that young man out of her head. His gaze, as if contemplating his beloved rather than a corpse. A languid joy at recovering a vestige of she who once was.

All afternoon, that look has haunted her. What images do. The power of photography.

This ambivalence suffused her as she dressed almost automatically for her dinner with Teresa, forgetting off and on that today they were celebrating the reopening of the restaurant in the port. Their happiness has a bitterness to it. This was one of the buildings most damaged by the flood. The water swept away everything. Even part of the façade. Dolores was certain this was the end of the business, as it may have been for so many that have yet to reopen. The ceremony is cheerful but somber at the same time: jubilation at the possibility of moving forward, sorrow at what's been left behind. The good fortune of a second chance, the satisfaction of perseverance. And buried beneath that, indignation. Dolores feels it. It's there in the pinched faces of the servers, the forced smiles, the tense posture, the way the dishes are laid on the table...it's subtle, but she imagines them fighting the whole time against some invisible force.

They're at their usual table, the one facing the window that looks out onto the sea. From there, they can see the aftermath of the flood, the mud streaking the walls, bits of the structure that broke away. Carlos, the owner, has decided to leave it that way. Along with the line marking how high the water rose.

"I don't want to forget," he told them before writing down their order.

They got the most expensive tapas, scallops, shrimp, wild sea bass, a fancy wine.

"This is the only way for them to stay afloat," Teresa said, raising her glass of Jumilla. "And we're alive, at least. Not like the dead people in your photos. Come on, tell me all about you and the old man."

Dolores described the commission, Clemente's house, his collection of mortuary photos, and delivering the pictures to the widower. She watched as Teresa's face slowly changed, until she erupted:

"I honestly can't understand how you got mixed up in this. I mean, my hair was standing on end just listening to you. Don't you think this is all a little crazy?"

"No."

"Well, I do. Very much so."

There's a pause, as though no more discussion were possible, then Teresa says, "If it's to satisfy your curiosity, fine. But to actually dedicate your time to this ... are you sure it's good for you?"

"Why wouldn't it be?"

"Maybe you don't need more dead people in your life."

"These dead aren't mine."

"Exactly. Don't yours give you enough to deal with?" She hesitates, then adds, "Or is it that you haven't seen enough?"

"What do you mean?"

"You know perfectly well what I mean."

"Don't go there, Tere," she cuts her off. She's not in the mood for that argument, not now.

"Sorry. But I just don't get it."

"You know I…"

"You couldn't. I know. And I do understand that. I still have nightmares about that night. But it's fine, we won't go into that right now."

"It's best not to." Dolores sighs and looks elsewhere.

She knows they still need to have this conversation, it's hanging over their heads. But not now.

The afternoon Luis died, she and Teresa drove together to Antequera Hospital, where they'd taken the body, on the A-92, toward Jerez. When they got there, Dolores broke down and couldn't enter the morgue. *I don't have the strength*, she told Teresa. And Teresa said she'd do it for her. She still remembers that day, that hallway, the waiting, the long minutes that she thinks sometimes gave birth to that dark absence that steals her breath.

When Teresa came back, they hugged but didn't say anything. Just that she'd identified the body. That was all Dolores needed to know.

"I did what had to be done," she remarked on the drive back. Dolores took that as a reproach. Teresa had been brave, she'd been a coward.

They've never spoken of the moment since. But Dolores has a hunch that what happened that late night gave rise to a hierarchy of loss between them. Her sister-in-law acted, faced up to the situation, and she remained stuck, immobile, paralyzed, in a wasteland she still hasn't found her way out of.

She may be imagining it, but it seems there was something in that moment, an air of superiority, that survives in the way Teresa looks at her. For that reason, Dolores understands her reaction to what she's told her this afternoon. She puts herself in Teresa's place and can see that for an outsider, especially for her, it's incomprehensible. And so she attempts to rein in the conversation:

"Don't worry about me. This is different. It's just photography. Really. I know what I'm doing."

"Sure," Teresa says, "nobody knows you better than you."

"You're right about that."

Teresa smiles softly. Dolores sees Luis's smile behind hers, but she's used to it. The open nostrils, the pursed lips, as if she were holding her breath, keeping something to herself.

"Instead of the dead, let's talk about the dying. Specifically a man I know who's dying. To meet you, that is."

"Excuse me?"

"He's the director of the Regional Photographic Archives."

Dolores doesn't understand.

"Remember the dentist I told you I had a crush on?" Dolores nods. "The other day we had dinner with a friend of his, Alfonso, the director, and for some reason or other, you came up. I guess I must have told him my sister-in-law was a photographer. His eyes were like saucers. Then I said you'd photographed a dead body and you'd met some old man that took these morbid photos and he was done for. You should have seen his face."

"You're probably exaggerating."

"He gave me his number and said we absolutely had to organize something. He's an elegant fellow."

"Teresa..." Dolores cuts her off.

"Just do it for curiosity's sake. What do you have to lose?"

"I don't know..."

"Look, Lola, curiosity's what got you into taking photos of dead people and now you're all wrapped up in that old man, right? Come back to the living for a while."

"We'll see."

"That's a yes."

"It's a we'll see."

6

IS SHE SURE ALL THIS IS GOOD FOR HER? THE anxiety her conversation with her sister-in-law provoked takes days to go away. It's just photography, she told her, that's all. But in her heart, she thinks there's something more there. Much more.

Teresa's words have made her think of that fateful night again. And of the day after. The viewing and the funeral. Her cowardice, her inability to look at Luis's reconstructed face. And the guilt. The awareness that in a way, everything had been her fault. The distance, the decisions. What she said, what she thought. What she can never tell Teresa. Or anyone else. What she doesn't dare to put in words. The absence condensing at her side.

Is all this good for her? she asks herself again. She doesn't know, but what she's sure of is it isn't bad. As she told Teresa, in the end, they're not her dead, and it's not her pain, she thinks as she develops the final versions of the photos of the dead young woman. She feels a slight but sharp pain as she imagines the widower receiving them.

"He says he wants them all," Clemente told her yesterday on the phone. "You have to let them choose. But they almost always hold on to everything that's left."

When she's done, she puts them in an envelope along with the negatives. She regrets letting go of something she's spent so much time with, and the feeling follows her as she takes everything to Clemente's, leaves it on the coffee table in the living room, and settles down on the sofa. He's prepared a black velvet album with a golden lock to present the photos. More than an album, it's like a reliquary, a shrine for a prized memory. He's always done it that way, he says. The factory that makes these albums still exists, he says, but in case they go under, he buys them forty at a time and keeps them stored away.

"I like the size, the texture," he says as he offers it to Dolores. "It's like caressing a body."

She reaches out and grazes the soft surface of the book. The trail of her fingers remains visible on the velvet cover.

Leaning his elbows on the table, he inserts the copies slowly and solemnly into frames that have been die-cut into the pages. When he's done, he slides the negatives into a small envelope on the last page and proudly shows the end result to Dolores.

She puts the album on her lap and notices how perfectly the photos fit their frames, and feels as though she's embracing a person. The images have taken on a different quality, more intimate, more poignant. It's the velvet, but also the grain of the photo on baryta paper, the materiality, the weight, and the presence. And the possibility of shutting it and keeping it for yourself, with a little metal closure that reminds her of the hasp and lock on a treasure chest.

"Do you want to stay for lunch today?" Clemente's question rouses her from her trance. "Vasil's making a moussaka. He always makes too much. I'm sure you'll enjoy it."

Dolores says yes. Once again, it's lunchtime and she hasn't bothered to get anything ready. She doesn't like to cook for herself alone, and when her son's not there, she winds up just eating whatever. And for a while now, the scent of onions and spices in the sauté pan have reached her, and they've awakened her hunger.

While the moussaka bakes, Dolores walks to the kitchen to help Vasil with the salad. Since the day he came to the studio to pick up Clemente's photos, they've barely exchanged a word. When he's with his employer, he usually remains silent.

"Is this dish . . . from your country?"

"From the Balkans. I make it like my mother cooked."

At first, it's difficult to get him to talk, but Dolores manages to find out Vasil was born in a small village near Burgas on the Black Sea coast and came to Spain ten years ago. Eight years or so after that, he met Clemente. His wife, Mila, who came with him from Bulgaria, used to clean Clemente's house once a week, and Vasil would come by to do odd jobs, construction and electrical mostly. He says he's a good electrician, but it's not easy to get steady work. Clemente was lucky Mila was there when he slipped in the shower. She was the one who called the ambulance and went with him to the hospital. She even stayed there with him through the night. But she had to get back to cleaning houses, and so Vasil came to stay with him. At the hospital, and later at home.

"He liked how I took care and Mr. Clemente hired me. I learn to do everything very fast."

Now that the old man's gotten somewhat better, Vasil goes home some nights or takes a few mornings off, but for the first few weeks after the fall, he lived there, escaping just a few hours to sleep at home with his wife.

"We're in this country to work. We came for that."

When they sit at the table, Vasil stops talking. Dolores notices his discretion. She can't help thinking of him as a butler. Clemente treats him amiably but not without condescension. He says:

"We get along so well because we both know what it means to emigrate."

As he speaks, he pours a few inches of wine into their three glasses and proposes a toast:

"To those who leave and find their place, and for those who return and accompany us."

Vasil cuts the moussaka and serves Clemente first, Dolores second, and himself last. He's made enough to feed a family. She remembers eating something similar with her husband on a trip to Paris. At a Greek restaurant in the Latin Quarter. She tells Clemente this when he asks if she's familiar with the dish.

"Paris..." he says. "I stayed much farther south."

And as if wanting to emulate Vasil's tale, he recalls to her how he set off as a young man to seek his fortune. He had just turned twenty-five, almost the same age as Vasil when he left Bulgaria, when he emigrated to France in the sixties. He landed in Gardanne, close to Marseille, where he found a job as a mechanic's assistant and practically never left. It was that village where he turned into—his exact words—a photographer. As soon as he could save some money, he bought a Leica III, which he used for years, and discovered his true vocation. There he met Émile, owner of the only photography studio in the town, a tall man, nearly seven feet. He paid attention to Clemente's photos, helped him trust his own eye. And eventually he offered him a job in his studio.

"Big Émile... he was the one who took me to photograph a dead person for the first time."

Clemente eats a bite of moussaka and takes a sip of wine. Dolores notices his skill at dosing out the episodes of the story. Before anyone can butt in, he continues:

"I remember that morning as if it were yesterday."

And as if it really had happened not long ago, scarcely eating, scarcely stopping to refill their wine, Clemente tells how one day he and Émile traveled to a hamlet in Gignac-la-Nerthe, near Marseille. The mother of a large family had died, and her daughters had asked for a photo. Émile's studio offered mortuary photography, though even then the custom was dying out. His father had been one of the most renowned funeral photographers in the region, and Émile had decided to keep the tradition going. As long as he could. Because, as he'd say later, he wasn't enthusiastic about it. It depressed him, and when he went to bed, nightmares pursued him. People then still held viewings at their homes, and you had to go there. In the smaller villages, everyone wanted a picture of themselves with the deceased, and the sessions dragged on forever. But at least there was no need to move the body, he said, it was already in the coffin when the photographer arrived. In Émile's father's day, the family would sit the deceased at the table or in an armchair. It took several people to move a body, and at times they had to break bones to get it into the right position. Émile saw this as an adolescent, his first years in the profession. The dry crack of the bones never left his head as long as he lived. He told Clemente that the first day they went to photograph a corpse, whether to frighten him or to tell him how much had changed since the old days, he didn't know. What Émile couldn't imagine was how those photographs of the end would fascinate the young Spaniard, who still struggled to hold a conversation in French. Or how careful his gaze was, how full of feeling, how much respect and affection he was able to transmit in his images. The beauty of their composition. Their technical perfection. In a few months, Émile started passing along all his increasingly rare commissions for mortuary photographs.

With time, he would leave the run of the studio to him. Until the day he retired, at least, and the business was passed down to his children. Clemente still worked there, but after a few years—enough for his children to realize that the studio brought in less money than they'd imagined, and they'd have to put in hard work for it to go anywhere—they turned it into a franchise, and everything changed. In place of the old, sober white, the shop was now garish green, the counters filled with backpacks, lighters, canteens, and travel items. They sold tobacco and chewing gum, made copies, and every day, Clemente had to put on a green vest and a transparent visor with the company's logo. What made him give up, more than any of this, was the feeling that photography no longer mattered there.

"I was a photographer, not a clerk. So I retired as soon as I could, left them there to traffic with their gewgaws, and, for the first time, I considered leaving France and coming back here. Spain was my country, after all. And there's always a time to return."

He's weary by the time he says this, and stops a few seconds to catch his breath. He's spoken with vigor, but his voice has begun to weaken. The story intrigues Dolores, but she's worried about the old man, who continues as though under some hidden obligation. He tells her how hard it was to adapt to Spain again, to the hours they keep there, the customs. He tells her how he struggled to keep that venerable photographic tradition alive. It disappeared here even before it did in France. No one remembered how they used to photograph the dead. Still, he arrived in the village and offered his services to all the funeral homes nearby.

At first, they didn't take him seriously, they thought it was macabre, bizarre. But one family opted for a portrait of their dead mother and received the velvet album at their home as a last memory, and then, people started looking at it differently. Word spread thanks to families who had done it and found it moving, and even the funeral home workers noticed that the photos gave comfort and helped people bear their mourning. The custom spread. To the extent that something like that can. He's never understood why more commissions haven't come along. Six or seven in the course of a year. Eight at most. But he's resigned to it. Anyway, he doesn't do it for money, he does it from conviction: the certainty that the photographs have meaning, that they can help those left behind.

"That's what I've always done, that's what you've begun doing with me," he says, looking at Dolores. "*Et c'est tout.*"

Tired, Clemente takes another breath, stops talking, and grabs his glass. As though celebrating the end of his story, he gestures to Dolores and takes a generous sip.

"Some story," she says.

Vasil doesn't react. Perhaps he's heard it all before.

"Some story, yes," the old man says drowsily. "The blink of an eye…*la vie.*"

Throughout, Dolores has been able to see the large daguerreotype hanging on the living room wall. Clemente's wife with their son in her arms. How old would she be there? How old would she have been when she died? Dolores hoped that she—the woman whose name she'd forgotten—would appear at some point in the story. But Clemente's spoken only about his relationship with photography, as if that had been the true motor of his existence.

She isn't sure whether or not she should ask, but finally she does.

"Did you meet your wife there? What was her name?"

"Gisèle. The promise. That's what her name means. I did meet her in Gardanne, not long after I arrived, and we married there too. Eric was born, and we made our home. Those were the good years. Later…" He clears his throat and fills his wineglass with water, which turns pink as it spills inside. "Later, things ceased to be the way they'd been before."

For the first time, Dolores sees emotion in his face: eyes damp, lips pressed together, hand gripping his chin.

"The illness took her away. The hardest thing was watching her vanish little by little. She barely got to enjoy this house. Here, too, life passed in the blink of an eye."

Dolores regrets asking, and she can't find the words to console him. And she realizes she hasn't seen Gisèle's mortuary photo. At least, she doesn't remember seeing it among those in his collection displayed in the vitrines. She imagines it must be in the album he showed her the day he visited the studio. The one with the images of the people who have meant most to him. She doesn't know why, but she has no doubt the photo exists. She's tempted to ask, but before she can figure out how, Clemente says:

"You, too, know what it is to lose the person you love most, don't you?"

Dolores responds with a look of resignation. She doesn't know if this is the time to tell that story. Probably not. So she condenses it into a few phrases. Her husband died in an accident. He had his whole life ahead of him. Those years weren't easy.

"It's hard to get past it," she concludes. And then, as if to put an end to any attempt to take the conversation further, she tries to get up and clear the table. Vasil stops her.

"Don't worry," he says. "Let me have your plate."

She remains seated, and for a few seconds she says nothing, not taking her eyes off Gisèle's portrait. The face now has a history. Clemente seems to sense what her gaze is getting at, and turns toward the image himself.

"Someday, I'll teach you to make a daguerreotype," he says, looking back toward Dolores. "As you can see, they're beautiful. Nothing is comparable to the magic of watching them come to life before your eyes. Would you like to try?"

"I'd love to."

"*Alors*, that's something else for us to do."

7

TERESA PARKS BY THE RIVER, AND DOLORES tells her she'll meet her at the restaurant in an hour. It's the first time in months Dolores has been to Murcia. She came early, planning to visit Iván at his apartment, but he said he'd rather see her for coffee in a bar close to the university.

It's not long before he asks about her photos and she tells him what happened at the funeral home with Clemente.

"Whoa," he says over and over.

When her story's over, Iván opens his backpack and takes out a thumb drive, which he sets on the table.

"I brought you a movie," he says. "*The Strange Case of Angelica*, by Manoel de Oliveira. You haven't seen it, right?" She shakes her head. "It's a little dark, but it reminds me of all this, because there's this photographer who has to take photos of a dead chick, and then he falls in love with her."

"I don't think this will go that far," Dolores responds, tucking away the drive and adding "I'll give it my undivided attention."

"Be patient. The concept's good, but the director's a drag."

Iván's comfortable, she notices, more self-assured as he talks, as though the city's bringing out the adult in him. She likes seeing him happy, at ease in the capital, as she sees on their walk to the restaurant. He knows all the shortcuts, doesn't waver, the city is his. He has a year of school left and doesn't know what he'll do when he finishes, but Dolores doubts he'll return to the village.

He leaves her in front of the place she's having dinner, a renovated old post office that's now a high-end food court.

"Mom, you're going to the most chichi spot in Murcia."

"Your aunt picked it. You know me, I go where they tell me to go."

"Great, have fun. And be careful on the way home."

Dolores holds their goodbye hug until Iván slips away and walks off toward the university. She watches him: he has his mother's hips, but his father's broad back and deliberate step, as if his body weighed on him and he had to be certain of each footfall. Before he rounds a corner, he turns and softly waves goodbye, probably knowing his mother's watching him. She stands there a few seconds after he's gone, not knowing what to do. She'd like to run after him, and she's tempted to, but instead she pulls herself together and prepares to go inside. She sees herself in the glass door. Her dress looks good on her. The dark pattern is subtle. Just enough to make her feel she isn't wearing a disguise.

The place is bustling, and so amid the tumult, she struggles to see anything. At last she finds them in the back, sitting at a high table.

When she reaches them, she says hello and sits on a barstool, her feet dangling in the air. She's always found high chairs uncomfortable, unstable. They make her feel like a ventriloquist's dummy.

A bottle of white wine is already open, with a dish of roe and dried tuna.

Her sister-in-law introduces everyone. She hates these moments, and she's afraid her face shows it. She's still thinking of Iván. She tries to return to the present.

Raúl is the dentist—orthodontist, he clarifies—that Teresa met at the Murcia health department. He has a kindly face that reminds her of a village priest of old, but his shaved head and trimmed beard add a note of sophistication. Seeing his smile as he pours the wine, she understands perfectly why Teresa fell for him.

Alfonso is the director of the Regional Photographic Archives. He's a more forbidding type, his stern face, his prominent widow's peak, and his refined bearing reminiscent of the actor José Coronado: correctly, he stands and greets her with a kiss on each cheek. His brown leather belt matches the coppery pocket square in his jacket. He's a deliberate dresser, tactful.

He takes the floor, addressing Dolores directly:

"Teresa told me you photograph the dead."

"Well, not exactly." His tone bothers her slightly.

"I say that with admiration. We have a few such portraits, old ones, in the archive. Honestly, I didn't know people still did it."

Dolores tells him she didn't either.

"Tell them about the old man!" Teresa interrupts.

She doesn't like the way she's said *old man*, or the fact she's said it at all. Grudgingly, she offers a few details: the call, the photo, the visit, his collection . . . She's curt—all this is private, and she doesn't wish to be disrespectful.

"It sounds like a movie," Alfonso says.

"I told you," Teresa responds.

Dolores realizes all of them are listening raptly. She hates that: talking to more than two people at a time. All those eyes looking at her. The conversation is vexing. And it's so noisy, she has to raise her voice, and she worries everyone at the other tables is looking at her. She tries to cut the tale short:

"We're not going to spend all night talking about dead people, are we?" She wants it to sound like a joke, but her irritation is evident. The physical discomfort may be making it worse. The lack of a chairback to lean on bothers her, and she can't figure out how best to sit.

But dinner doesn't take long to arrive. When it's over, Alfonso says they should have a nightcap elsewhere.

"Just make it somewhere comfortable," Dolores says.

El Parlamento is a different story: a place out of time. Luis took her there more than once, but it never did quite jibe with her. She used to joke that it looked like a place for English lords. The same waiters as always are there. The elegant décor is the same, too, the wood paneling, the cozy wing chairs. When she settles into one, she has to stifle a moan, a wince. It's the years, she knows. And the time she spent taking care of her father. He was deadweight, she had to move him on her own, and when it was over, her back was shot. She notices it most at the end of the day. The physical burden and the other one, the one no one can see. Day after day. The weight of the world.

In the years since, she's recovered, but at certain moments the pain concentrates in that same old place, which is a magnet for her body's malfunctions. Sitting so long on the stool in the food court revived her old aches, and the deafening noise, the nerves, made it worse.

Relaxing, she places her purse on her lap to mark the distance, and orders a ginger ale, making an excuse to the waiter:

"Someone's got to drive."

They don't stay long, but it's long enough to see the attraction in Teresa's and Raúl's eyes. The faint lights there are an invitation to gather close. The waiter pours Alfonso a Lagavulin Special Release. He takes a sip and pulls his chair closer to Dolores.

"Has it been long since…you know. Teresa told me."

This question normally bothers Dolores, who doesn't feel she should have to reveal such things.

"Ten years."

"The time never passes, does it?"

Dolores nods.

"The only person I've lost is my mother, years ago, but sometimes, without my knowing why, it all seems to come back. It goes, but it comes back. That's what mourning does."

"Yeah," Dolores says dryly. She's not upset, but she's also not in the mood to linger on the subject. Alfonso seems to realize this and turns back to photography, telling her about the archive and inviting her to visit.

"Anytime you like. You can even tell…"

"Clemente Artés."

"Yes. I'd like to meet him. See his collection one of these days, if possible."

"I'll see what I can do."

His tone is different now, less distant, as if he no longer needed put on a show. She likes how he looks at her. She's never known how to interpret men's attitudes—she was always the last to know when a guy liked her—but she senses desire in Alfonso's way of addressing her. She caught him looking at her legs earlier, when they were walking to the bar. And she didn't mind.

"I saw how he was looking at you," her sister-in-law tells her later, in the car. "That dress really suits you."

"It's probably the expensive whiskey he ordered."

Much as she'd like not to, she can't help comparing every man to Luis. The Luis she knew, the one she spent half her life with, until the two of them were one single person. The Luis who hated stiff, gentlemanly manners, who disliked sophistication, the natural, genuine Luis who was no different in public than in his living room. Over time, Dolores made his stance her own and internalized that contempt for refinement and gallantry. But when she thinks about it, she doesn't exactly mind being treated that way. For too long, she's been a caretaker, a mother, a widow. Not a woman. Let alone a desirable one.

That night, she sleeps more serenely than usual. She doesn't think of Alfonso. She doesn't even know if she likes him. Probably not. But she can't get his eyes out of her mind. And she likes that feeling. She understands

Teresa now, her going out, her need to not disappear. Because that's what it's about. Being visible. For ten years, Dolores has been gone. Frozen. Cold. But tonight, something awoke. She feels the heat emerging slightly. Senses it. For a few moments, at least. Until the dark absence bursts in and reclaims its place.

8

SHE'S NEVER SEEN THE BACK PART OF THE house before, the frowsy little yard and the shack with the fiber cement roof that was originally intended as a garage. There, in his workshop, as he calls it, Clemente has readied the daguerreotype materials for Dolores.

"It used to be less of a mess, obviously. The few times I did use it. I hope you don't mind the state of it."

"I don't," Dolores says, surprised by all she finds there. The equipment looks like something from a museum, and she wants to apologize for making him go to the trouble of dragging it all out.

"It's a shame it was ever put up," he says.

Much of what this *it* refers to Dolores can't identify: there's the camera with the accordion bellows, which she had seen in the house and had assumed was just for decoration; wooden boxes, cloths, a torch, trays, bottles of chemicals…it's more a laboratory than a workshop. A run-down laboratory, with folding tables and plastic chairs. Clemente sits in one and begins to describe the process.

Much of what he says is familiar to Dolores. Any photographer worth their salt knows the story. The origin of photography. The dispute between Louis Daguerre and his nephew, Joseph Nicéphore Niépce. The purchase of the patent by the French state. The invention that changed the world. The technical and mental transformations it inaugurated. Images that came from a mechanical eye without human intervention. Unique images, relics, magical, alchemical, brought into being by mercury vapors. She knows all that, sort of. But as she hears Clemente's words, it acquires solidity.

He talks to her about the technique's lineage and the origins of her vocation. He refers to it as a genealogy full of failures and dead ends. The daguerreotype stands at the beginning of photography, but it was quickly abandoned for quicker and more economical techniques. Wet-plate collodion. Calotypes, which turned photography into a multiplier of images: the negative, the paper print, the copy. How all this developed slowly into the photography industry as she now knows it. The very thing that is now ceasing to exist. A path she undertook with Luis, which something else is superseding. She knows this. She's lived it. And a part of her remains behind on that short path.

She's heard the story. But she's never touched the original materials. And seeing them there now is like entering a magician's secret chamber.

"It's nothing special," Clemente tells her. "It's just craftsmanship."

Much of the equipment he's made himself, especially the wooden boxes. It wasn't hard, neither is the process. At least for someone who knows it well. Three steps: prepare the plate, take the photo, develop it. All it takes is time and practice.

"And lots of patience," he concludes.

As he talks, Clemente prepares, on the folding table in front of him, the chemicals he's poured into small glass jars. The dense, bitter vapor recalls the pesticides in the recently fumigated orchards she passes sometimes on her morning walks. Chemicals and the morning dew.

Dolores watches the old man at work. He moves everything skillfully, but slowly, appearing to reflect before each step.

You start, he says, with the sheet of silver-plated copper. Today they're using a quarter-sheet, the most popular size: 108 by 81 millimeters. The full-size plate, 216 by 168 millimeters, was only rarely used. The daguerreotype in the salon, of Gisèle and their son, is a full-size plate, he says, polishing and burnishing the silvery surface until it gleams like a mirror. Then he places it face down in a wooden box with a pane of glass and exposes it to the iodine already inside. He repeats this action with bromine fumes and then returns to the iodine. The fumes and the mix of halogens and silver enable it to capture the light.

"Now the alchemy begins," he says. And he turns off the lights, leaving only the red laboratory light burning.

Every ten seconds, he checks the color of the reflection. At first it's yellow, then it turns pink. When he gets the tone right, he inserts it into a frame and switches on the lights.

"All this," he says, "for a single image. We don't have this kind of time these days, do we?"

Dolores nods. Most people would despair at how long the process requires.

Now Clemente takes the camera with the bellows she had seen in the living room before, the museum piece, it seems to her, though it's simply a camera obscura and a lens.

"We're returning to the essence," he says. "Here, help me."

They walk out to the yard. It's eleven in the morning. There isn't a cloud in the sky.

"It's a lovely day. What do you want to photograph?"

Dolores looks around, trying to find something she'd like to see reproduced on the plate, but all at once, everything strikes her as both extraordinary and too insignificant to appear in such an image. She reflects for a moment. As she was entering the development, she noticed a house at the end of the street, half-built, now in ruins. She mentioned it to Clemente. He liked the idea.

"We'll give it a sixty-second exposure," he says when they reach it. "And keep in mind, you know, the image will be reversed."

She arranges the camera atop the tripod and, following his directions, opens the bellows and tries to frame the image and adjust the focus. But it's hard to see in the sun. She understands now why photographers used to cover their head with a black cloth.

Once it's centered, Clemente inserts the plate, pulls out the protective slide, and removes the lens cap.

It's a subtle transition. There's no click, as with a traditional camera: the exposure simply begins. Rather than capturing an instant, they are revealing a process. A condensation of time.

They are silent for sixty seconds as the image impresses itself on the plate, as though their voices' echoes could slow or interrupt the process.

When enough time has passed, the old man covers the lens and slides the cover back over the plate.

On the way back to the workshop, Dolores notices he has difficulty breathing.

"Are you all right?" she asks as they arrive.

"*Très bien*," he says, slumping in the chair he sat in before. "I'm anxious to get to the magic part." He smiles and puts on latex gloves. "Which is also the dangerous part."

There are as many techniques as there are photographers, but he still follows Daguerre's original method, developing the image with mercury fumes, which yields more precise details.

"Isn't it toxic?" Dolores remembers reading that some of the early photographers poisoned themselves.

"As long as the quantities are right, there's no danger. This little ball of mercury," he says, showing her the bottle, "represents the contents of four thermometers, and I've had it with me since I arrived in Spain."

Early photographers, he says, used as much as a kilogram, sometimes more. It's no surprise they lost their minds.

"Poor Daguerre spent his old age convinced that the world was about to end and that he had to photograph it before it disappeared."

Delicately, he pours the mercury into a small receptacle, which he places in the bottom of a wooden box, somewhat larger than the others, on top of a small heater. He turns off the lights, and in the red glow of the darkness, removes the plate from its frame. Before placing it over the box, he shows it to Dolores and says:

"This is where the magic truly happens. Nothing here, nothing there."

It's true, the plate is bare, containing only what photographers refer to as the *latent image*.

The plate stays there for three minutes. He times it. Then he lifts it and shows it to Dolores. There's a faint outline. It needs a longer exposure. He places it back over the box.

"You can never be certain the image will appear. That, too, is magic. The charm of uncertainty."

Dolores tries to memorize the process, noting each step in her mind. She knows how to give things the time they need, and she's good at following steps, but learning something the first time is always difficult.

As the mercury draws out the image, Clemente pours liquid into three trays. This is more familiar to her.

He lays the plate in fixer. The half-built house is starting to take shape. He submerges it in the stop bath and turns on the lights. Now she can see it clearly. She's observed similar processes for half her life, but nothing has ever felt like what she's just witnessed. She begins to grasp what it must have meant to the first photographers to develop a picture. A pure transmutation of matter.

A few minutes later, Clemente bathes the plate in distilled water, and after drying it, he shows it to her. It's ready, but there's one more step. Gold toning, he calls it. He places the plate over a small metallic arm, spills a gold chloride solution onto it, and heats it with a wick.

"The gold seals it. Otherwise it's so fragile, a butterfly's wing could wipe it away. It also immobilizes the mercury. It's a protective layer, like varnish on a painting."

Dolores imagines a shifting image trapped by gold, light etched into the plate by fire.

"*Et voilà*," he says, handing the finished product to her. "Your first daguerreotype. *C'est simple comme bonjour!*"

She watched the building's outline appear bit by bit, but it's only when she holds the plate in her hand that she sees it's real. They both look at it closely, searching for the ideal angle to see it in positive. For a few tenths of a second, Dolores is confused by what she sees. She recognizes the picture she took, but at the same time it's strange to her, as though it had come from another time, rendering the home's calamitous state still more palpable. Behind it, in the very back, she notices another structure, the skeleton of a never-finished hotel. She'd overlooked it before, but she sees it clearly now: a future severed, a time to come that is now the distant past.

To prevent oxidation, the plate must be hermetically sealed, but Dolores takes it home as is. It's just an experiment, after all. And she likes the idea that this picture, like the ghostly house it depicts, is also destined to become a ruin. She thinks this at night before going to bed, with the daguerreotype in her hands, toying with it. She feels its materiality, its texture, its weight. For the first time she's aware that it had no prior existence, that she's the one who created it. And it now occupies a precise portion of space.

She can't stop looking at it, moving it to see it without her face reflected in it. A mirror with memory, she says to herself. She understands this metaphor better than she ever has.

9

FOR DAYS, DOLORES LIVES WITHIN THE OSCIL-
lating image of the daguerreotype, feeling the same attraction she felt when she first discovered photography.
When her mother bought her a camera, one of the first
Instamatics. It looked like a plaything, but it took good
pictures. She wouldn't stop asking for it, and her mother
finally gave in. It was her Communion present. Or that's
how she treated it. It was supposed to be for the family,
so they'd have a camera at home, but after Communion,
she kept it as her own.

Her uncle Emilio, her mother's brother, was the one
who always took the family pictures. Including almost
all the instants from her childhood. Dolores is smiling
in none of them. She wanted to be on the other side of
the camera. She remembers the feeling perfectly: she was
mesmerized by him, his posture, the way he drew the
image into focus. That was why her expression was so
strange: instead of posing, she was examining the maker
of the image, eyes squinting, lips pressed together. It's

the same face she makes now, fifty years later, whenever something grabs her.

She hasn't forgotten the attraction, the enchantment of everything pertaining to that tiny machine. She spent hours rapt before the pictures it took, which were themselves a tiny treasure.

She's found herself recently examining the daguerreotypes with the same fascination she felt for those photos. She wants to know more, learn everything, master the technique, control that magic.

And this compels her to return to Clemente's home and repeat the process. This time, she prepares everything. She didn't take notes, but her mind had let nothing slip: not the polishing, the sensitization, the timing, the placement of the plate in the camera...

Today, she will take a step further, face the true challenge with the daguerreotype: the portrait.

They go to the garden, and Clemente settles into a plastic chair near the balustrade bordering the street. The lighting's good. Forty seconds of exposure might do today, he tells her. It's not a long time for a landscape or an object, but for a portrait, it's an eternity. This is why, for many years, photographers relied on all sorts of devices to hold their subjects' posture. Clemente doesn't have any from that time, but he has made a rudimentary apparatus with the foot of a lamp and two spoons screwed together like a clamp. Dolores adjusts the back of his head until it's straight. Then she arranges the camera in front of him, and before sliding in the plate, sees him inverted on the focusing screen, and asks:

"Can you hold it?"

"Like a dead man." He smiles. "They're always better subjects than the living."

"Sure. They don't move."

"Almost never."

"What?" she asks.

"The dead," he replies. "They almost never move."

The phrase remains floating there in the air. She doesn't know how to respond, and after focusing, she inserts the plate, removes the dark slide, motions to him, and uncaps the lens. She tries not to look at him. The forty seconds expand, as if time refused to proceed.

The dead almost never move.

She can't stop thinking about that. Soon after, as she develops the picture, Clemente tells her what he meant.

It's the first time she's heard talk of the unquiet ones.

III

THE UNQUIET ONES

· · ·

1

"THE UNQUIET ONES. PHOTOGRAPHING THE process of death. Expiration. Dying condensed into an image."

In the room's red shadows, everything is vaporous. Dolores listens as she continues working with the plate. Clemente is sitting behind her. His hoarse voice echoes between the four walls.

It's portentous, as if revealing a secret kept for centuries. Or so it seems to her. But it's not exactly a secret, he says. It's obscure, but not entirely unknown. Émile was the one who first told him about it. *Les remuants*: the restless, the agitated, the unquiet—he likes this last translation for its antiquated ring. The practice—he emphasizes he's talking about a *practice*—evolved alongside postmortem photography, but goes beyond it. It's not a portrait of the dead, but an image of the process of dying. Remember, he says, the long exposure times of early photographs didn't show an instant, life frozen, but passage, duration, reality as it happened.

For Dolores, this sounds like the plot of a mystery. Especially when, with a coldness she can't quite grasp, Clemente tells her how these photographers allegedly worked. He says it was common to administer a poison to the subject that would *extinguish* him—what a strange choice of words—while the camera captured the arrival of death in the course of exposure. A concentrate of *Clostridium botulinum*, which he pronounces like the words of a spell, would produce permanent paralysis, usually terminating in death. The difficulty was to find the right dose to inhibit the body's movements. Because death always comes like a whiplash, twisting and convulsing the body. It was almost impossible to suppress that final spasm.

Dolores wants to let him finish, but she can't restrain herself.

"You're talking about murder!" She doesn't look at him as she exclaims this.

"*Bon*, if you find it consoling, they were usually on the verge of death. In a sense, you could call it documented euthanasia."

"I don't find that consoling." She looks back at the sheet of silver-plated copper and checks the time on her watch. Despite this turn in the conversation, she remains attentive to the development process, and it is close to time to turn on the lights.

"Don't let it distract you," Clemente says. "They were basically just experiments."

His voice has changed. Perhaps he regrets how coldly he has told her all this. He counters that the first photographers were chemists, doctors, researchers, not so much artists, and that what they were exploring was above all the technique's scientific applications. These photographs of the unquiet were taken not for families, but in the furtherance of knowledge, and tried to show, on a single surface, life and death, the last breath, even to trap the soul of the deceased, record the invisible, the *élan vital*.

Dolores can't help but think of the spirit photography of the nineteenth century. She's always felt drawn to it, but she's never truly understood it. The ghosts of the dead posing alongside those who survived them. When she mentions this to Clemente, he tells her that the industry in question was the furthest thing from the photos of the unquiet ones.

"Spirit photography was the terrain of swindlers who took advantage of the gullibility and pain of their customers. They were charlatans, but they were pioneers in retouching and image manipulation."

The photographs of the unquiet ones, he continues, represent a tradition true to reality rather than illusion, born of the attempt to ratify the one certainty, which is death, gathering in a simple image its before and after. Preserving life and death in one place.

Regardless of the intention behind these pictures, they were almost inevitably disconcerting. He realized this when he held in his hands a daguerreotype Émile's father had acquired at the beginning of the century. It was unsettling, the contrast between certain very clear details and others so vague as to be indiscernible: the outline of the subject, the sheets, the curtains, possibly windblown. The body was stationary, apart from the slight movement of its breathing, like the intangible palpitation of living beings when they are photographed alongside the dead.

"Unfortunately," he concludes, "few of them have been preserved, and they're practically impossible to get hold of."

Dolores thinks of the image she found in the book Clemente gave her. It's been in her head the entire time he's spoken, and she can't help asking him, "Was that one a..." She doesn't know what to call it. "An unquiet one?"

Clemente waits a moment, as though unsure how to respond.

"It's possible," he says hesitantly. "Or it may simply be a daguerreotype that was moved during exposure."

"Is it also part of your collection?"

"It was. *Malheureusement, je ne l'ai plus avec moi.*" Dolores waits a few uncertain seconds, until he clarifies: "I lost it."

"Good," she replies. What she's hearing upsets her, and she tells him this as she extracts the plate from the developing box and lays it in the tray of fixer. "I don't like this story."

"You're right not to," Clemente says. "But imagine possessing life and death condensed forever in a single image. An artifact of the final traces of existence. What better remembrance is there? Would you not like to die in a photo?"

Dolores doesn't respond. She's dizzy and terrified, and she senses that her face may show it. The mercury vapors. The lack of ventilation. The iodine, the bromine, the scent of fixer mixed with the old man's aroma. In that space, his tale is too dense, too real.

She stops moving the tray of fixer and turns on the lights, which is a way of escaping what Clemente has just said.

She looks at the image.

The old man's face is a blur.

"You moved," she says as she shows him the plate.

"Just as well," he replies. "That means I'm not yet dead."

2

SHE SEES THE IMAGES FIRST ON TELEVISION, then on her phone, in a barrage of WhatsApp messages. They're everywhere. Thousands of dead and dying fish, struggling to breathe, on the banks of the Mar Menor. They cling to the back of her eye, bringing to mind images of the first Gulf War, dying cormorants soaked in petroleum, or the *Prestige* disaster. Horrors that took place far away but are now happening a few feet from home.

A disaster! A disgrace! A tragedy! These expressions are repeated in every conversation: in her messages to Iván, in her words as she talks on the phone with Teresa about what's happened.

"Something's got to be done," her sister-in-law says. "I don't know what, but something."

"Something," Dolores repeats. "It's a disaster! A tragedy!" She can't emerge from the spiral.

At night, it's hard for her to sleep. It's the effect of what she's seen, and the feeling of impotence. Plus her unease those past few days. She hasn't slept well for a while, actually. Not since Clemente mentioned the unquiet ones. That story has wormed its way into her dreams.

When she got home, the day she took the daguerreotype, she opened his book and turned to the last page. That image had disturbed her the rainy night when she first found it, before she knew what it was. Now, she does, and the mist surrounding the body laid out on the bed upsets her more intensely. Clemente had said it might just be a movement during exposure, but Dolores sensed the throbbing in it. It shook her, the thought of holding that fragile object in her hand, seeing her face reflected in the material residue of the moment of a person's death.

That night, she walked down to the studio and tucked the book away in one of the cabinets in the small storage room, as if in this way to hold at bay whatever it was she'd seen. And she found herself on the internet searching in every possible way for *the unquiet ones*. There were hundreds of pages of postmortem photography, but none of them offered any insight into what Clemente had told her. She was surprised by the morbid reflections in the texts she discovered. On the screen, everything was much more obscene: exposed to the eyes of any and all, unsupervised, unsettled, unquiet in its own way. She understood why Clemente housed his photos in a velvet album. It was a way of making representation material, something that could be touched, embraced, like a body.

She found thousands of images in cyberspace. But nothing about the unquiet ones. Nothing about the photographic tradition Clemente had mentioned. Just before closing the computer, she clicked on several articles referring to funeral rites intended to calm the unquiet dead. In many cultures, it was common to place stones over the dead or even nail them to the ground with bronze spikes: magic spikes that kept them from shifting and returning to the world of the living, huge stones to make the earth lie heavily upon them.

Despite her best intentions, the thought of the unquiet dead remained moored in her memory as a corpse was moored to the earth, a portrait moored in the copper of a daguerreotype long after its subject had expired.

Fettering the dead to keep them dead. Fixing a memory. There was something macabre in the practices of these cultures she had read of, and yet, in a way it made sense. Because for her, the memory of Luis remains unfixed, floating, also unquiet. There is an absence around him, a darkness that remains impenetrable to her, outside a concrete space, while she is anchored, feeling one of those immense stones weighing down on her, or magic nails pinning her eternally to her past.

She hasn't ceased to think about these things since. But she's said nothing to Teresa or Iván. She hasn't felt like it. She doesn't want them to think there's something wrong with her, that she's doing something she shouldn't. For days she's been unwell. And the sight of the dead fish today has only worsened her angst.

As she tries to sleep that night, they join together: the futile flopping of the fish on the banks, the mortal agitation of the person in the photo, and the dark absence that takes away her breath—an inquietude in the interior of her dreams.

3

THE NEXT DAY, BEFORE HER MORNING WALK, she throws her camera over her shoulder, instinctively, the way she did when she was twenty, with the vague notion of photographing the scene, documenting it, peering at it through the viewfinder.

It's cold out for August, and she's glad she wore a jacket, jeans, and close-toed shoes. She walks to the beach where the fish appeared. She intended to hurry there, but her camera has slowed her down. Everything around her is a possible subject.

The village is like the set of a disaster film. Weeks have passed since the rainstorm, but the evidence is still all round, and on that morning, more than ever, it resembles the wreckage of a ship. *I don't want to forget*, Carlos said when they asked why he hadn't repaired the flood damage in his restaurant. She doesn't want to forget either. And she's decided to photograph everything.

When she met Luis, Dolores always had her camera around her neck. The Canon AE-1 she had bought with her savings. It was her passion. And it may have been what got Luis to notice her. It wasn't common, a girl her age with a professional rig. That was the start of their relationship. Luis never admitted it, but the camera, and the way she used to crouch down to frame a scene, were what turned her from his sister's friend to Dolores—his Dolores.

"You've got him hooked," Teresa told her the day after she had left the two of them walking on the shore. "He calls you the girl with the camera."

She remembers the early years. He liked to teach her. He seemed to enjoy it. And she was a good disciple. She learned how to use the light. That especially. Luis used to jokingly call her *Lolita, light of my life*. He was seduced by that urge of hers to capture everything around her.

When did that end? She's asked herself more than once. She's asking herself today, as she carries the camera slung like a purse over her shoulder, ready to document the remains of the disaster. She can't remember why, exactly. It just happened. She got up one day and didn't feel like taking it with her. That set a precedent. And the days added up.

When they opened the studio, they divvied up the roles. He was the photographer, the artiste. She was his helper and stood behind the counter. He looked through the viewfinder. She developed. He was the professional, she was an aficionado who went around with him and enjoyed his work. That was how things had to be. She had to stand aside and let him show off. Perhaps that's why she wound up exiled to the studio, the way she'd once been exiled to the kitchen at the bar. ID photos, developing, indoor work. She never thought of it as giving something up. It was a choice. But one that slowly killed her enthusiasm and stunted her gaze, and she withdrew, as though she never wanted to leave there again, or didn't know how. Until now. Until recently.

She hasn't thought it over a great deal. It's just that she feels the need to stand behind the viewfinder. It must have something to do with the past few weeks, her realization that photos matter. The way they used to matter to her. The way they used to matter to Luis. And then there's her gift, her gaze. The one that Luis once saw, that faded, and that has risen up again. That special gaze Clemente said she possesses, and that makes her notice all that's around her.

When she arrives at the beach, it's full of people: journalists, residents, rubberneckers, disaster tourists. Some with cameras, most with phones. What's strange, more than the sight of it, is the silence: the whispers, the muffled words that leave audible the futile flapping of the fish.

She walks away from the crowd. The beach's broad expanse is covered in fish. She sees sole, gray mullet, red mullet, sea bass, sea bream, steenbras, eel, shrimp, crustaceans of all kinds. It looks like the counter at a fishmonger's, but dyed a grotesque, filthy green by the algae and water. Contaminated, murderous water.

Anoxia. She heard that term on the radio, and it's stuck in her head. The water doesn't have enough oxygen. And so the fish come to the surface to breathe, and they die there, or they're washed up on the shore, where they breathe their last breath.

The Mar Menor is a cemetery. She read this in the press. Everybody's looking for an explanation. It's the cold drop. The fresh water from the ravines. The contamination. Especially the contamination. Nitrates from the farms. There's more of them now, but they've been draining off for years. Intensive agriculture. Treating the earth like a pantry. All these things, and nobody willing to take the blame.

She readies her camera for a panoramic shot. Instinctively, she loaded it with black-and-white film: the old man's words stuck with her. She kneels on the sand to capture a detail, focusing on the lifeless eye and open mouth of a bream.

It screams into the silence. She feels she can hear it through the viewfinder. Constant, droning, high-pitched, drilling into the top of her head.

She stands back up and shakes the sand off her pants. That sound, that shrillness, lingers, along with the feeling of dizziness. It happens every time she kneels down; she needs a few seconds for everything to return to normal.

She takes a few more photos, and realizes what she's capturing is mourning. The mourning of the fishes, but also of the sea. And in a sense of the village too. The thought recurs to her as she goes home and sees the closed shops and the signs of flooding—signs of an end that she feels the need to document. She feels driven to preserve the moment. To keep from forgetting. To stop time. Like those magic nails that pin the dead to the ground.

More days like this follow as she recovers her routine. Reawakens to the world around her. In the morning, at midday, at night. At different hours, under different lights. She photographs the village in the wake of the catastrophe, the village she's lived in for a long time without seeing. She'd hardly noticed how everything has changed in recent years. Because looking is one thing, and seeing is another.

———

She runs into her on a Friday, sitting at a patio table in front of the marina. She stands and greets her. Dolores doesn't recognize her at first, even if her face is familiar.

"Don't you ever let go of your camera?" she asks.

Only then does Dolores realize this woman is the daughter of the dead man she saw in the funeral home last August. She doesn't remember her name, but she still recalls how uncomfortable the woman was as she was photographing her father.

"Ascensión," she says, introducing herself.

For courtesy's sake, Dolores asks how she is.

"You get used to everything," she says. "But I miss my father. You never think, *OK, he's old enough, he can die now.*"

"It's hard. With time, though…"

The woman asks:

"How were things with the old man?"

"Clemente?" Dolores corrects her.

"I hope he didn't gull you too."

"I don't understand."

"Don't get involved in his obsessions. That nonsense about photographing the dead…I don't know why I let him do it."

"Remembering our loved ones," she replies, as though citing Clemente from memory, "isn't just nonsense."

"No, it's crazy. It's the kind of thing a crazy person does. No wonder nobody wants him around."

Dolores shrugs and frowns. She doesn't want to argue. She wants to end the conversation and go back to shooting in the port. The woman seems to understand, and softens her tone.

"Anyway...I just wanted to say hi. But be careful."

"Don't worry."

"And ask him one day why he's so alone. I'm curious what kind of rigmarole he comes up with."

4

SHE TRIES TO FIND THE RIGHT MOMENT TO ASK. But on the way to the funeral home, she can't. She picked up Clemente early in the morning and they've taken the highway to Cartagena. The building is at the end of one of the first exits, on the edge of town. The trip lasted just over thirty minutes. He spent them telling her the details: a woman collapsed suddenly at home. The burial's this afternoon. One of her children hired them.

Getting out, she turns and wonders: Will this ever stop feeling like a film to her? Clemente walks straighter than last time, but his labored breathing shows even the first few steps tire him. She follows him with the tripod, the camera and equipment in her backpack, always one step behind. She helps him climb the stairs, and they walk into the vestibule together. At the desk, he asks for the family of the deceased, while she notices how diaphanous the room is, the orange glow, the exposed brick walls and the concrete pillars, the composite flooring made to look like marble, the round skylights, the red plastic chairs arranged in groups of four...it could just as well be a doctor's office or the waiting room in a government building. A space like any other: antiseptic, neutral, abstract, with no particularities. She's never been there, but everything's familiar.

The funeral home where she held services for her mother and Luis was a large one that served all the towns on the coast. The one in the village, in the industrial park there, hadn't yet been built. Her father's service took place in the new one. But her memories get mixed up. Her mind can't quite tell them apart: both are empty, soulless, incapable of mitigating loss. Concrete, iron, and brick. Indistinguishable sofas and armchairs. She has the feeling such buildings are impervious to pain. A house is different: it accompanies those left behind. She felt that when they held the wake for Nana Reme at home: the space itself was weeping, and at the same time it healed, lulled, protected them from the pain. She never told anyone this, but she would have preferred to do the same with all her dead. She's always hated rushing them out of the place where they once lived, to get rid of them as soon as possible. Out of the house, out of our lives. So they don't contaminate us with their presence. Carting them off to the middle of nowhere, to abstract structures made to render memory uniform.

In that indifferent building, Dolores and Clemente walk to the room the employee has indicated, and just as she did the first time, she observes his every movement.

Again, she's struck by his serene expression, cool and warm at the same time, both with the man who greets them in the hallway and with the other children of the deceased.

"I share your pain," he says. And this expression seems to be the right one.

There are four siblings there, but only the youngest one asks if he can stay with them. Clemente says yes, and the three of them enter the room where the body's kept. Dolores buttons her leather jacket. She's cold, and even the dense, sweet scent of roses and carnations is sharp as ice.

She hadn't meant to gawk, but she can't help it this time. The woman's face is flawless. She doesn't know why, but she tells herself she didn't suffer. If she had, her face would preserve some remembrance of pain, and there is none. Just a slight yellowing of the skin, a resolute terseness, tells her it's a dead body. She thinks of all those clichés people utter in front of a corpse: *That's him all right. Just as he was in life. He looks like he's sleeping.* All this she could say about the woman in front of her.

She tries to calculate her age. A little bit over seventy. The son who's stayed with them is young. Not even thirty. Even if his black shirt makes him look older.

Clemente and Dolores respect his silence, whispering a few brief directions to each other. And they try to work fast.

"Get in and get out," he told her the last time, and that stuck with her. "We're interrupting their mourning.

For this brief period, imagine we're in their home, and we can't overstay our welcome. Imagine how it was when we used to go to their houses. Here, it's like we're part of the staff, that makes it less uncomfortable."

But Dolores can't escape the feeling that she's impeding another person's grief. At the same time, she imagines what she's doing brings some small sort of relief, that any activity, any movement in that inert space brought to those stagnant hours the promise, at last, of movement.

As she helps Clemente, she realizes the young son is attentive to their every gesture. As he looks at his mother, she can't avoid putting herself in the place of the deceased. Imagining her own death. She's thought of it before, though never in front of a corpse: What would happen if she left Iván behind? That fragility is hard for her to imagine. She doesn't suppose she'll live forever; to the contrary, death is always on her mind. But she's been convinced, for years, that she can't leave him. Iván can't bear another loss—that's what she's told herself. She can take the pain, the deaths, her mother, her father, Luis...but she can't go herself. That's what terrifies her most: leaving her son. If she doesn't obsess over it, it's because she can't conceive of her own end. She'll always be there. She'll be there for Iván. All the time that he needs.

When they leave, the young man thanks them and then hugs his three siblings. Dolores watches from the corner of her eye as they reach the door. The children's suffering. She uses it as an excuse to ask something she's wanted to ask for a long time.

"They look very close," she tells Clemente.

He nods, struggling with his seat belt. And she asks him outright:

"Has it been a long time since you've seen your son?"

He hesitates, perhaps not expecting the question, and responds:

"Too long."

She wants to know more. But the subject is difficult for him, and his answers come only with reluctance. His name's Eric, the same as his grandfather on his mother's side. He still lives in Marseille. He works in a bank. He has two daughters. Or maybe more. Clemente doesn't know, because he hasn't seen him since Gisèle's funeral.

"That was eight years ago now. Hard times those were."

"Does he call? Does he care about you? Do you call him?"

"We don't get along well, if that's what you're asking. Nor is there really anything to say."

"A father and son, though," she begins, but can't find a way to end this phrase. "Does he know you're...?"

"How I am?"

Dolores pauses. Alone and sick, she wants to say, but she holds her tongue.

"That you're far away," she finally says.

"He knows everything he needs to know."

"But…"

"Look," he concludes, to draw the conversation to an end. "Every family is a world. And every world is a story, and not everyone can understand it. *C'est tout.*"

Dolores thinks she's crossed a line, and decides not to go on digging. Clemente falls silent and looks out the window. It's hard for her to remain quiet. It's funny: she's always fled noise and chitchat, which reminds her of her parents' bar, but the distance between two people who sit next to each other in silence, that universe that opens between them, their private ways of being lost, gives her vertigo. She knows silence is necessary sometimes, but it discomfits her. And maybe to bridge the gap, she decides to tell him she's been photographing the effects of the flood on the village and that she's been shut up in the laboratory developing these pictures for several days. The work is slow and laborious, but pleasant.

"I'd like you to look at them," she says.

"Sure," he responds. "*Avec plaisir.*"

The way he says this tells her the waters have settled. She says she has some with her in the car. He tells her to have a coffee with him at home, where he can look at them at his leisure. Everything is fine.

5

SHE INSISTED ON MAKING THE COFFEE HER-
self. Clemente was wearier than usual when he got
home. She helped him into his chair, and after putting
the transparent folder with the photos on the sofa, she
brought him a glass of water.

"We said we'd have coffee," he remarked. "I'll make
it right now."

"Don't worry, you relax. I'll take care of it."

The kitchen's small, and everything's easy to find.
The bag of coffee, closed with two clothespins, is in the
first cabinet she opens; the cups, turned upside down,
are next to the sink, and the coffeepot is under a faded
red rag. She doesn't brew it too strong. She doesn't know
how well it will sit with him.

While it's boiling, she looks for milk and sugar. The
sugar bowl is on a shelf in a closet that serves as his
pantry, which has endless cans of soup and other foods
stuffed in the back. The refrigerator is almost empty.

A milk carton, a plain yogurt, a wedge of cheese, and three eggs.

Seemingly reading her thoughts, Clemente shouts a justification from the living room:

"Vasil has to buy groceries this week. I told him already. Don't worry about me going hungry."

A few minutes later, Dolores returns with the cups, the sugar—she found no artificial sweetener—and the coffeepot on a tray. She's usually discreet, and it surprises her how readily she's gone through his things.

Clemente has opened the album and has a few pictures on his lap.

"They're lovely," he says after Dolores serves him. "And strange."

"They're disaster images."

"*C'est vrai*, landscapes of mourning. And yet there's beauty there. And art. Above all, art. The way you look at the world…"

"They're the first ones I've taken in ages…just on my own, I mean."

He looks a while longer, as if wanting to root out what's inside them, and she likes his studious way of proceeding. Luis used to look at her photos like that, too, back when she shot everything around her and he praised her ability to find the most unexpected perspectives, the least-evident side of things, piercing the surface and revealing what lay there but was invisible at first glance. She had done this in her photos of the flood's aftermath in the village, and in those of the dead fish on the beach. The images are fresh and demand slow contemplation. Three steps of looking, as Luis used to say: a first glance to understand what that unusual point of view reveals; a second to relate it to one's own experience of its object—to things already seen; and a third to recognize that image and experience never completely coincide. A complex way of looking, that thinks and makes one think. She never formulated it in these words. It's just how she took pictures, how she approached things, from the least predictable angle. After lying dormant so many years, that approach was dead, she'd thought. But now, when she sees the concentrated look on Clemente's face, the intensity and attentiveness, she realizes nothing is ever lost forever, and there are things you can't forget. She's pleased to feel that reawakening within her.

"They're powerful, Dolores, they really are."

She remembers that the plastic folder also contains negatives that didn't turn out. Blurry, dark, underexposed...She tries to dissuade Clemente from looking at them, even to close the folder when he reaches them. But he grabs her hand and stops her.

"I like these too," he says.

"They're failures."

"No image is a failure."

She likes how that sounds. He lets go of her hand and looks at the photos a bit longer. Then he gets up, very slowly, and tells her to come to the room that houses his collection. He wants to show her something. She follows him, noticing how he drags his feet.

"I didn't show you the entire collection," he says, opening a large wooden armoire in a corner. "This is where I keep my archive of failures. You're one of the few people I've shown this to."

Some of these pictures he's bought, but most are his own, he says. Then he sits in the chair in the center of the room and tells her to look at whatever she likes.

She carefully opens a few cardboard folders. She finds in them half-finished pieces: scratched, torn, smudged, crossed out. Proofs. Images without an image. Landscapes, families, events, portraits, even mortuary photographs. Some make her think of the unquiet ones, the photo in the book. But what she feels has nothing to do with that. She's not disturbed, rather the opposite. These pictures bear the imprint of nostalgia. They are lost worlds, each of them. Clemente's words confirm this:

"They're keepsakes, made for someone they never reached. Orphans, in that sense. I like having them there, all together, keeping each other company."

She's grateful for his words, and for showing her something so private.

"Take all the time you need," he tells her.

She takes a few minutes more, then they return to the living room. She follows him down the hallway, and holds one of his arms while he sits on the edge of the sofa. He doesn't speak as he tries to recover from the effort.

"Vasil will be here soon," he says. "It's time. You can go whenever you like."

"Are you sure you're OK?"

"I'm just tired. *Je vais très bien*. Don't worry."

But she's worried. She can't help it. And she takes as long as she can gathering her things, hoping Vasil will arrive before she finishes. She slips the photos into the folder slowly and puts it in her bag. Ignoring the old man's protests, she takes the cups, the coffeepot, and the sugar bowl to the kitchen. And she washes the coffeepot unhurriedly in the sink.

When Vasil arrives ten minutes later, he finds her there with her jacket sleeves rolled up and her blouse spattered with water.

"I didn't want to leave him here," she says softly.

"I take good care now. Thanks."

His words ease her mind. She rolls her sleeves back down and walks out, passing the sofa, where she grabs her bag and says goodbye. She isn't sure for a moment how to do so, but at last, she puts a hand on his shoulder.

"Keep well," she says.

He turns to her and smiles, with a grateful expression that gives her a knot in her stomach.

6

WHERE DID THAT COME FROM? SHE ASKS HER-self in the car on the way home. But it isn't hard to say. She knows that needy, defensive look better than any-one. She struggled with it for too many years. And she didn't think she'd ever see it again.

She can't say what happened between Clemente and his son, but no one escapes their responsibility toward their parents. She never did, she accepted it to the very end, even when it would have been easier to stick her father in a nursing home and be done with it. She had already helped her mother take care of him when they diagnosed him in mid-2004. It won't be overnight, the doctor told them, it will take a while, but your father will cease to be the person you knew. He'll fade out, vanish, one bit at a time. She remembers how hard that day was. They cried as if he'd already died. She consoled her mother. She'd be there for anything she needed. Iván was only five, but she'd find a way to help. She had faith in her mother, and was convinced that, despite her weight and the ulcer on her leg, she was strong and could take care of him to the end, an end that wouldn't come for a long time, but that they'd begun to accept. But life's events don't follow a program, and just over two years later, she fainted in a supermarket and there was no reviving her. Her heart had exploded.

Something exploded in Dolores too. She had lost her mother and had to care for her father. There was no way around it. But she had Luis's support. And he knew she had no choice. He's your father, you're an only child, it happens, of course you've got to do it, you can't leave him on his own. He recommended they rent out the house in the village when they put her father's bed in the room where they did their ironing and stored their junk. The extra money would make things easier.

At first, Iván enjoyed being close to his grandfather. But no one knew how hard Alzheimer's was or how fast the changes come. The doctor hadn't prepared them for that. In a few months, her father was someone else, especially when night fell. It's because we moved him in here, being in a different house has thrown him off, they told themselves. He'll get used to it and be back to his old self soon. But he never did get used to it, and his old self vanished forever.

Her privacy was gone. And her life with Luis, too, in a way. Even before his death. She's thought that many times, hat those years were when they began to pull apart. Those empty years, as she called them, not yet knowing they were the last ones. The years when she was a mother to her father, a mother to her son, but not a wife to her husband.

Luis never reproached her. But it was clear that things weren't working at home. He didn't tell her he couldn't stand it, that they'd made a mistake, that they couldn't live that way; they could, it just meant living differently from before. Giving up, giving in, disappearing.

That was when Luis bought the motorcycle he would die on. A friend was selling it because he never drove it. It was a deal, and anyway, he could pay it in installments. One afternoon, he showed up on the Yamaha V Star, parked it in front of the studio, right by the window, and walked through the door in his leather jacket with a helmet under his arm.

She remembers it well, that flash that for a moment brought back to her all the happiness of the past. He'd been on a motorcycle when she'd met him, that was her very first impression of him, and that afternoon, for a moment, it was all there again: the springtime of life, falling in love, uncertainty, passion, freedom. But the flicker died, and she understood that the past had returned, but only for Luis.

Motorcycles had been his life. He couldn't believe he had gone for so long without riding one. He needed to get back that youthful passion. So he argued. But she knew all he wanted was to escape. Flee the dark house, the television cranked up to ten, the locks on the doors, the adult diapers piled up in the bathroom, the contagious stench of old age. She'd have liked to escape too. But she stayed there and heard the Yamaha roar off and vanish in the distance, and in herself, in her solitude, she roared as well: Make something happen to him, a little accident, just enough to screw up his plans, just enough to make him come home.

She thought that on the last day of his life. Wished for it, more than she ever had. He was spending the weekend in Jerez with friends, enjoying life, actual life, while she tended to her father and held their home together. He had an entire weekend away from that black hole, away from her.

I wish this thing with the motorcycles would end, that you'd accompany me in my misery, that your happiness would turn to sorrow.

Her wish came true.

And the guilt never went away.

She chastised herself for thinking that, and for everything else too. If they hadn't brought her father there, maybe Luis wouldn't have bought the bike, the distance wouldn't have come between them, she wouldn't have wished for the accident, he wouldn't have died. She blamed herself, and she couldn't help but blame her father too. That lasted for some time after Luis died. The empty years, she'd called the time when her father was living there and Luis had pulled away from her; the years between Luis's death and her father's didn't even possess the status of time. They were a time of mourning postponed, but with no one shoulder to cry on, no rest to absorb the loss, a time of fiction, a fiction maintained before her father, as she concealed her suffering. On some days, she wanted to talk to him, to share her pain. But she would look into his lost eyes and realize there was no point.

Six years of grief suppressed, six years of gradual weakening, for her as well as for him. When he died, she could finally breathe. She hadn't hoped for it, but every day he survived was like imprisonment, an intermission. For many things, but especially for mourning for Luis. That could only begin afterward, and it had lingered there, an obligation ignored.

She still hasn't emerged from the mourning, the gathered suffering, a life mortgaged and handed off. That's why the coffee she made Clemente today meant so much. Why the old man's defenseless gratitude gave her a knot in her stomach. She can't help empathizing with solitude. But she's already suffered for her own people. They were her responsibility. He isn't, and she can't shoulder the burden, she thinks as she drives back home and tries to rebuild her armor. She's had enough. Clemente isn't her problem. He shouldn't be.

7

YET AGAIN, SHE ROLLS UP THE BLINDS IN THE studio in the morning for no reason. Today, not even a confused passerby has stopped in to see if she makes copies or sells pens and notebooks—she's never understood why they think this. Sitting behind the counter, with the radio playing in the background, she savors the empty hours. She needs nothing more, she tells herself. And she tries to find an excuse to duck the evening's commitment. A few days ago, she promised Alfonso she'd visit the photographic archive, and despite her better judgment, she agreed to have dinner with him too. She thought this would give her the chance to see her son, if just for a few minutes. But last night, late, Iván told her he'd be spending that day at a friend's house in the country. It popped up out of nowhere, it's a surprise party. I'm really sorry, but you understand. Of course I do, she assured him. But her world collapsed, and she immediately wanted to cancel or postpone her visit to the archive. She thought this when she went to bed, and she was still thinking it when she got up.

She'd like to be firm, efficient, tell Alfonso no. She repeats this to herself after her nap, getting grudgingly in the car and driving toward Murcia. It's not the first time she's done something she doesn't want to do to keep from inconveniencing others. She's burning inside, but can fake it and put on a kind face. More than once, her abilities as an actress have alarmed her.

"We're closed to the public this afternoon," Alfonso says, opening the door for her and greeting her with a kiss on each cheek. "So your visit will be even more special."

As he walks her down the hallway, he tells her how the archive works. It's managed by the regional government for the purpose of preserving the local photographic heritage, principally through restoration of old pictures. He's been the director for two years, tasked with keeping the project afloat. He's still getting to know the collections.

After several narrow corridors, they reach the conservation room, small, walled in opaque glass panels, full of machines whose function she doesn't know. A strong scent pervades the room, but she can't quite place it.

"We're used to it," Alfonso says. "But it's not pleasant, I know."

Two young people with face masks and white coats are restoring photos. Interns from the university, he tells her. They look up to acknowledge her.

He guides her elsewhere, stopping in a gallery with high ceilings, closets, metal shelves, glass cabinets with restored photos on display. In the middle is a large table.

"This is the inner sanctum," he says. "Where we keep everything. And of course, anyone who wants to can come in for consultations."

They sit down, and he shows her a large book bound in red velvet.

"This is an important project. *The Regional Photographic Album*. A selection of photos. It's one of our most recent publications. I wrote the text." Before she can even look at it, he adds, "It's nonsense. A trifle."

"The book's lovely," she says as she leafs through it, stopping at several old pictures of the city.

"I spilled blood, sweat, and tears to get hold of some of these old collections. You can't imagine what a headache estates can be. Especially widows. They're the worst."

Dolores looks at him, briefly stunned.

"Sorry," he excuses himself. "I . . . I'm just saying."

"I know."

"Wait," he says, changing the subject. "This you'll find interesting."

He stands, opens a drawer, takes out a series of photos in plastic envelopes, and lays them on the table. Photos of the dead. Dolores inspects them with curiosity.

"Fernando Navarro," he says. "One of the historic photographers of the region. His family did it all. Built coffins, arranged flowers, even took the body to the cemetery. An all-inclusive package."

Dolores listens to this ironic explanation without taking her eyes off one of the photos. A group of people gathered around a woman's body, all in mourning. The living look more dead than the deceased. What especially attracts her is the perspective of the countryside. Most of the pictures like this she's seen—the ones in Clemente's book, and others she's found on the web—are French, English, North American, and show middle-class people in period clothes. They feel far away. Whereas these are folk scenes, death up close, even as it is distant in time.

As she looks, Alfonso brings her a book about the photographer.

"In case it inspires you. It's another of our publications."

He also gives her a small book of photos from a private collection.

"I managed to acquire them after negotiating with a collector. Where better than here for such things!"

She thanks him and places it on top of the others. The pile is now growing large.

"No worries. I'm going to get you a bag."

Alone, Dolores opens the book he's just given her. After the prologue by Alfonso, she sees a picture of him with the collection's owner, smiling, content, a wily hunter posing with his bested prey.

"That collection was a major find," he tells her, returning with a paper bag. Sliding the books inside, he asks, "Do you think we could convince Clemente Artés to donate his?"

"It's not up to me to say," she replies without thinking. "But I doubt he'd be interested."

"Would he at least see me? Could you mention it to him? I'm asking as a favor."

The request is a bit pushy, and for a moment she isn't sure how to respond.

"I guess it won't be a problem," she finally says.

His self-assured expression unsettles her.

At the restaurant, Alfonso greets the waiter, who takes them to the back of the dining room, where a corner table is hidden behind a small white screen.

"I requested this table in my reservation. The owner's a friend. He's going to make us something special."

Alfonso doesn't open the menu. There's no need to, unless she wants something special or has any allergies they should know about.

"As you wish," Dolores says.

He asks for the owner and tells him to make whatever he likes. But not to leave off the shrimp croquettes, the razor clams, or the pork belly *ssäm*. As for the wine, the same Jumilla as last time, but the 2017 if possible, that was a good year for the winery.

She doesn't quite buy Alfonso's routine, his combination of decisiveness and extreme diligence. He's the furthest thing from Luis, who always let her pick, who never had any idea what you were supposed to order where, and who generally struggled to make decisions. He took forever to choose his dishes, except when they went out with Teresa and her husband. Then, Dolores would take the lead and always knew what to ask for. If Luis was on his own, he always waffled. Only with photography was he ever certain. Daily life, on the other hand, he found exasperating, a nightmare, whether it was decorating the house or the studio, choosing a pair of pants or shoes, even figuring out what to watch on TV or at the movies. It got on her nerves sometimes, but there was something tender in that irresolution. It wasn't so much doubt as the acknowledgment that not everything had to be known right away, that there existed a right to uncertainty.

Alfonso acts like he knows everything: where to go, where to sit, what to order, what wine pairs with what dish. Naturally, that makes things easier for the person next to him, who just has to sit back and follow along. But all that self-assurance makes her uncomfortable. And amid that discomfort, from a desire to stand up for herself or to show that she knows something too, she's surprised to find herself asking:

"Do you know about this tradition of photographing 'the unquiet'?"

"What?"

"The unquiet," she repeats.

"I have no idea what you're talking about."

That's the first thing he doesn't know this evening, and secretly this pleases Dolores. Without really knowing why, she repeats everything Clemente told her about the practice. She tells him about the picture in the book and the unease it transmitted, though the old man told her it was just that the subject or the camera had shifted. As she talks, her satisfaction turns to anxiety. She's revealing something private, betraying the trust Clemente placed in her. This is clear when she sees Alfonso's open eyes, his astonished face, his rapt expression.

"Fascinating," he exclaims. "It's the first time I've heard of such a thing. It reminds me of *Peeping Tom*. The camera capturing the instant of death. I love that film. You must have seen it."

"Yeah," she seems to remember, though she can't be sure.

"It sounds like a snuff film. I know someone who will find it fascinating. A colleague from the master's program in Madrid who..."

"Let's not, OK," Dolores interrupts him, hoping Alfonso will soon forget it. Maybe it's too late. But she tries to change the subject. "We should move on to something else. It's your turn."

"For what?"

"I don't know. Tell me about yourself." It surprises her that she's being so direct. "What you did before you were running the archive."

She barely cares about the answer, but she breathes easier as the conversation takes a different turn. She feigns attentiveness, as she knows how to, learning that he studied geography and history but couldn't get a job at the university because he didn't have an in. This was the perfect excuse for him to move to Madrid, where he learned about the art world from the inside. The real world. He worked at a gallery for ten years, and even opened his own company, managing cultural events. It didn't go badly, but everything comes to an end. It's the same for moments in your life. He's referring to his twelve years of marriage, his two daughters, who are practically women now. He shows her a photo. They look like him. He returned to Murcia after the divorce just as the former director of the archive was retiring. Alfonso had management experience and contacts. From the real world, from Madrid. This was his first time at an institution like that, but it ran itself. Functionaries, he jokes—they make things function.

"This will last however long it lasts. In the meantime, I'm trying to enjoy myself and do something worthwhile."

Dolores now feels obliged to talk about herself. Which she hates. Telling your life story, going back over it, summing it up, turns everything into an anecdote. She can't imagine anyone would be interested in hearing what she has to say. So she tries to be quick and pick out the most relevant details. How she dabbled in photography, studied art in school, met Luis, opened the studio, how they made a name in the village, her parents' death, Iván's birth...

"And the accident, you know."

Dolores says this almost unmoved. She already talked about it on the night they met. She doesn't want to again. Doesn't want to say it, doesn't want to feel it.

Alfonso responds in monosyllables. She's not trying to make him uncomfortable. Him or anybody else. That's how she is: don't bother, hide your pain. Even with Teresa, it's hard for her to bring it up. Her mother was the one who showed her how to conceal your suffering, how to keep it all to yourself. That was what women had to do: be prudent, be quiet, endure.

Later, Alfonso asks her about the photos:

"What exactly do you feel when you're standing in front of a dead stranger?"

It's a disingenuous question, and she doesn't like how he's phrased it. She thinks he's both picking back up their unfinished conversation and making a veiled reference to Luis. She doesn't care for him drawing a line from her photography to the death of her husband. She's dissociated the two in her head, as with the death of her parents. Her subjects are the dead from elsewhere, not her dead, as she told her sister-in-law. She could repeat this to Alfonso. Just as she could tell him about the armor she's built around herself, how it seals her in and is probably the reason she feels nothing. She's asked herself, these past few days, the same thing he's asking her now: when she's standing by the dead bodies, but especially when she's with the children, the husbands and wives, the brothers and sisters. She knows she'd fall apart without her armor, that's the answer, she dons it and she feels nothing, or tries to feel nothing. But she keeps this to herself, responding:

"It's hard. Really hard."

"It must be," he replies.

When the waiter leaves the check, Alfonso refuses to let her pay, throwing his card down on the metal tray and looking at her smugly.

"You don't have to do that."

"It's the least I can do. You came to see me." He folds the receipt in half and slides it in among the many slips of paper in his wallet.

Outside, the October chill greets them, the damp of autumn nights. She feels it especially on her cheeks.

They walk to the parking deck below the plaza by city hall. Barely anyone is on the street. Alfonso keeps his distance the whole time.

"Are you all right to drive?" he asks when they get there.

"I barely had a drop."

They stand a few minutes beside the white Corsa, while Dolores looks for her keys in her purse. She notices her fingers are trembling. She's forgotten what to do in these situations. She just wants to get in her car and go home. Among other things, she feels a pressure in her bladder and doesn't know if she'll make it.

Alfonso takes her hand and brings the back of it to his lips.

"It was a pleasure, Dolores."

"Likewise," she responds, blushing, but relieved that it's stopped at that.

She gets in and starts to maneuver, with Alfonso guiding her out. Before she pulls off, she's surprised to hear a knocking on her driver's-side door.

"The collection!" Alfonso shouts. "Don't forget to mention it to Clemente Artés. You'd be doing me a huge favor. I need something like that for the archive."

8

NO, SHE FEELS NOTHING. SHE DIDN'T TELL AL-
fonso, but that's what happens in the refrigerated room
in the funeral home while she's setting up her equipment
near the deceased: she thinks of no one, hears no one,
hides behind her armor, that shell that grew around her
with Luis's death and that she can sometimes feel physi-
cally, like a weight, a curved stone pressing down on her
chest. It makes her feel safe, imagining it that way, even
if she struggles to breathe beneath it. With her armor,
she can do anything. She feels less, but feeling less means
not feeling pain. Her pain or the pain of others. She tells
herself she can control it, make it thicker or thinner, and
that she decides when to put it on and take it off. Or she
used to say that, but then a day comes when her armor
shatters into a million pieces.

Three years old. Bone marrow cancer.

On the drive to the funeral home, she can't yet imagine what's about to happen.

"This one's not like the others," Clemente warns her. "If you want, I can take care of it. You can wait for me outside. It won't be easy."

But she insists. And her insistence ruins everything. Even before she sees the tiny coffin. It's the feeling there, the extreme reserve and respect. Outside, even the habitual mumbles and whispers are absent. It is desolation distilled, the silence after the cataclysm.

She tries, again, to take solace in the old man's presence. But it doesn't help. Sorrow surrounds them. She feels a pressure in her head, the air weighing her down.

The boy's parents receive them. A young couple. Not even thirty, probably. The father can barely look at them. It's the mother who speaks.

"Thanks for coming," she says. "We want to remember him. We had him so briefly..."

Her composure is devastating. She must be on pills. Or maybe she simply can't accept it. Maybe she only looks like she's holding it together, the way Dolores did at Luis's funeral. She didn't break down then. That must be when her armor started taking shape.

The idea of what's happening there fills her eyes with tears, affecting her even more than what she sees when they open the door to the cold chamber and the chill sinks again into her bones. It's the idea, not the sight of it. Because the little body just looks like it's asleep. More so than any she's seen. The mother notices this and says:

"He's sleeping."

It's impossible to think otherwise.

"Asleep in a garden," Dolores says with a sigh. They try to cover up the coffin.

They move the flowers. The room is full of them. She's never seen so many before. There are enough of them to hide the small white casket, making it seem, to her eyes, as if the boy were hovering among the wreaths and bouquets.

Clemente shows Dolores where to place the tripod and the reflector. His attitude is warmer than usual. He must know what's passing through her mind.

He works like a scenographer, his face exhibiting grief, his eyes dry, whereas Dolores keeps weeping despite her attempts to control herself. She pants, clenches her teeth. She's struggling to remain professional. She doesn't want to break down in front of the mother.

"They're the ones who are suffering," Clemente had told her when they were first working together. "You can't take their pain away from them."

But when she sees the scene set and imagines it as a photo, she feels a tear stream down her face, tastes the salt in it, and her jaw clamps down even tighter.

"Put the reflector there," Clemente tells her, "to shine some light on the face."

His words sound curt in that frozen room. Anything but an expression of agony would.

The mother observes the ritual. The father remains outside. Dolores comes close to the boy's face to brighten it. His thin hair is parted to the right, like a little man's. Did his mother do that? She remembers the photos from Clemente's house. Particularly the small daguerreotype with the lock of hair on the other side of the frame. And the way he told her the hair was a relic, and the photo, too, a sign of the presence of a being in the world. She read that in the book, that the majority of mortuary photos were of children. Children died easily then, but there was this idea current then that those there was no picture of had never existed. Memories of fleeting life. Less a *memento mori* than a *memento vitae*.

Little angels, they used to call them. The flowers around them, the body slightly elevated. Little angels rising up to heaven. She's familiar with those photos, and they've always upset her terribly. But nothing she's seen prepared her for what lies before her in that icy room. The creative process no longer shields her. She's a part of the scene. She can't find a way to dissever what she sees and her emotions, herself and what is lying there in front of her.

Her professional concentration in no way distracts her from the implications of what's happening. It's not just a photograph, a subject: it's a child. A future broken, a life aborted, the testament to the meaninglessness of everything that she can imagine—the meaninglessness of a tragedy like this.

She holds it together until she gets to the car. She purses her lips as she says goodbye to the parents. She hangs a few feet behind Clemente, walking slower than him, unable to hold back the pain and coordinate her movements at the same time. She opens the trunk of the Opel Corsa and drops her backpack and the tripod inside. She helps Clemente into the passenger seat, closes his door, and stands there a few seconds, eyes lost, leaning against the car. And she begins to cry disconsolately. She wishes she could have held on till Clemente was home, but she can't help it. It bursts out of her, and there's nothing she can do to stop it.

The old man doesn't get out. He can probably guess what's happening, even if he doesn't bother to look. Nor does he say anything later.

"I'll take the photos to the parents. Or Vasil will. Don't worry." Apart from that, silence.

Nor do they converse any further that day. It's the first time she's showed her vulnerability in front of him. She drives, throat inflamed, eyes fixed on the road, trying to contain her tears. Clemente respects her unwillingness to talk. Even his labored breathing grows stiller. She feels him next to her, feels grateful, his presence comforts her. But she needs to get him home so she can be alone. She needs to explode. And she does, once she's free of him. Her tears return forcefully. Not just because of what she's just seen, no: the tears are from elsewhere. From the suppressed grief of recent years. The floodgates have opened, her armor has fallen away. And behind it, her heart is red and raw. She feels it palpitating, scraped and scratched, can almost feel the blood draining from its wounds.

At home, she sits in front of her computer and searches for *angels postmortem photography*. She doesn't know why, but she wants to see those images again, and there they are, stretched across her screen. As if the children in those photos could push away the real corpse she saw in front of her. She looks at the settings, the depth of field, the vanishing point, the foreshortening, the number of figures, the composition... Attention to form somehow attenuates emotion, like a barrier protecting her from reality. She thinks. But slowly, something within her begins to stir again.

The worst thing is seeing those little creatures alone, defenseless against the camera's gaze. Very rarely do they lie cradled in their mother's arms, or between their parents, looking alive, asleep. When the mother does appear, it comforts her, despite the forbidding subject, to think the child is consoled, accompanied, in death.

What she's used to is mothers present, calming their children, even if they're invisible, outside the frame. She remembers what Luis told her when they started taking pictures of children at the studio. Shoots of babies. That their mothers soothe them. Often they had to stand behind the camera and look at them, making faces so they'd smile and keep facing straight ahead. Imagine how hard it was before instant cameras, Luis had said. You had to do something to keep the child from moving. And it became common practice to hide the mother behind a curtain or chair, cover her with a sheet or a carpet like a ghost, pretending to be a recliner or a divan, so she could hold the child unseen. *Hidden mother photography*, it was called. There was a whole tradition of it. Luis showed her some of those photos. They were ghastly. She remembered seeing one of her own mother as a girl, with her grandmother hiding behind a wicker chair, face turned away, trying to escape notice, as if playing hide-and-go-seek or some other eerie game.

Today she looks at them again. She types *hidden mothers* and watches them try to disappear before her eyes. Women hidden, women trying to stand aside. Invisible mothers. Camouflaged, staged. And she can't help but think how, for a long time, she disappeared too. Taking care of Iván, taking care of his father as if he were her son. Out of frame, out of sight. Keeping company, taking care, holding out. Sustaining others, with no one sustaining her.

She closes the computer and dials Iván's number. She asks how he is, and if he needs anything. If he's coming next weekend. She hasn't seen him in three weeks.

"I'm sticking around here," he answers. "We've got friends in town from Madrid and it's a little hectic. You don't mind?"

Of course she minds. But she keeps this to herself. She doesn't tell him she needs him, she wants to see him, hug him, hold him. She doesn't blackmail him emotionally, as he always accuses her of doing. Today, she saw a future cut short. Iván has his future, all of it, in front of him. He should live without worrying about her.

"Have a good time, Son."

"Thanks, Mom."

IV

PHANTASMAGORIA

. . .

1

ALFONSO IS COMING TO PICK HER UP EARLY IN the afternoon. She waits for him outside the studio, leaning on the window, nervous, even irritated at this visit she's set up.

The sun's bright and a little warm, and as she waits, she takes off the gray wool sweater she slipped on over her printed blouse. Alfonso doesn't take long. At the agreed-upon hour, a black Mercedes, which reminds Dolores of a car from a presidential motorcade in a movie, stops in front of her, and he invites her in.

"You can't imagine how grateful I am," he says as she eases into the passenger seat.

"It's nothing," Dolores replies, taking a few seconds to find the buckle to her seat belt.

She's never been a car person, but she can't help noticing the details, the tan leather upholstery, the wood texture on the dashboard, the big navigation panel in the center.

"It smells new" is the only compliment she can think of.

"It's not even a month old. But it's already started talking. Watch: Mercedes, take me to Clemente Artés's house."

As he looks at the screen, a woman's voice responds, "Right away, Alfonso. Starting route."

Dolores smiles, unimpressed.

"I already punched in the address you gave me. It's not that smart."

"I figured." She imagines Alfonso spent several minutes setting up the GPS before leaving just to impress her or make her laugh. She doesn't know whether she finds it funny or self-important. But at least she doesn't have to pay attention to the road and give him directions. She doesn't like being copilot.

The warm, artificial voice of the Mercedes guides Alfonso out. He tells her:

"For days now, I haven't been able to stop thinking about what you told me. The unquiet ones. The whole story's fascinating. I've been looking into it."

Dolores gives Alfonso a surprised look as he mentions an old friend of his from school, now a photography professor at the Complutense University of Madrid, who told him there were references to such a thing in nineteenth-century sources, but they were probably just old wives' tales. He knew of no photographs that proved the practice ever existed. And so he was deeply intrigued by the image Dolores had seen in the book.

"Maybe you could scan it or snap a photo on your phone and we could send it to him."

"I don't know if Clemente would agree…"

"He wouldn't need to know. I'd tell my friend to be discreet."

"Fine," she agrees, interested at the same time she wishes she'd never mentioned it. When they reach the house and Alfonso parks, she says, "Please, don't bring any of this up."

"Don't worry," he replies with a smile. "I'm quiet as the dead."

Inside, the introductions are brief. Vasil opens the door for them and accompanies them to the living room, where Clemente is waiting. He heaves himself out of his chair to say hello. Before he can sit back down, Alfonso places a paper bag with the logo of the archive on the sofa and begins:

"Dolores told me you have a wonderful collection. I can't imagine why we've never met."

"It seems Dolores likes to talk," Clemente says, glancing over at her as he falls back into his chair. She pretends to smile, but guilt starts to eat away at her inside.

He offers them coffee, which Vasil prepares, and shows them the room that serves as his museum.

"It's a modest collection," he tells them, opening the door.

Dolores hears less enthusiasm, passion, or sincerity in his words than the day he first invited her in. Artés says nothing about the cabinet with the flawed photographs. And the large daguerreotype of his wife and son is no longer there. When she glances at him out of the corner of her eye, she sees he's looking back at her. They are sharing a secret, she senses. And she need say nothing more.

Alfonso keeps asking for details. Technical data. Number of photos. Years. Formats. Media. Provenance.

"Is it catalogued?" he asks at the end of his inquisition.

"In my head it is."

"Fascinating," Alfonso exclaims. This is his catchword. Dolores has heard it before.

He examines a few of the pieces in detail, and they return to the living room. Vasil has left the coffee on the wooden coffee table in front of the sofa.

"I hope it's not cold," Clemente says.

He's the first one to bring his cup to his lips. Dolores does so afterward. It's cold.

Alfonso takes a small sip, puts his cup back down, and asks Clemente:

"Have you considered donating it? We could conserve it and catalogue it at the archive."

"*Pas du tout!* Absolutely not. I like being surrounded by my photos. I've spent my whole life with them."

"It needn't be now. But if you haven't thought about what you'll do with it..." He hesitates. "When you're gone."

"I'm not sure I care to think about that."

Dolores doesn't intervene in the conversation, which is cordial despite the evidently uncomfortable situation. The last thing she wants to do is upset Clemente.

"Don't answer me now. It's just a proposal. But if you do ever decide to donate it or even just lend it, the archive would be more than happy to store and catalogue it. Me especially."

Clemente tries to get comfortable in his chair, but can't find the right position. He groans softly, winces, the fatigue is evident on his face. Dolores knows it's time to go, and she starts the farewells.

"It's gotten late, no?" she says. Instinctively, she gathers the coffee cups and takes them to the kitchen.

When she returns, Alfonso's still sitting there. Before rising, he opens the bag he left on the sofa and takes out several of the archive's publications, leaving them on the table and pushing them toward Clemente.

"This is what we could do with your collection."

The old man thanks him and pushes the books aside without opening them. He tries to get up, but Dolores motions for him to stop.

"You don't need to see us out."

They shake hands goodbye. Alfonso first, then Dolores. Clemente holds her hand for several seconds and looks her in the eye. His eyes follow her out of the living room, until she turns the corner into the hallway. She realizes this when she turns to say another goodbye, but she doesn't know what it means.

On the way back, Alfonso asks, "Do you think we can convince him?"

"Honestly, I don't know," she replies begrudgingly.

"We'll have to let him think it over. But then we return to the charge. A collection like that, it's a shame for it to be lost."

Dolores exhales and looks out the window. Alfonso asks her what kind of music she likes and she says she doesn't care, whatever he puts on will be fine.

"Mercedes," he orders the car, "play John Coltrane."

The velvety texture of the sax and the soft chords of the piano flood the car as it floats over the highway. For a moment, Dolores imagines she's in a jazz club, and her discomfort vanishes.

Alfonso thanks her for the visit once more as he drops her off. When he brings her hand to his lips, he leaves it there longer than on the night he took her to dinner.

"You're fascinating, Dolores," he whispers. Then he comes closer and kisses her lips. She kisses him back, spontaneously, before pulling back and getting out of the car.

"Thanks for everything," he says.

"Good night," she responds, trying not to let her voice crack.

She's agitated as she opens her front door. Inside, she stands there thinking. Like a teenager. She didn't expect something like that to happen. She'd like it to stop there. But she can't help her body's quivering.

She hasn't felt something like this since Luis's death. Just as her feelings were closed off, her body had been closed off too. The armor over her heart also covers her flesh. No one has touched her for ten years. She's barely even touched herself. And so it's strange that night when she undresses and the silk of her blouse sliding off gives her goose bumps and her body reclaims its place. She slips her hand into her panties and places a hand on her sex. She isn't thinking about Alfonso, even if his body attracts her. What he's awakened is something abstract. Her orgasm is strange. Purely physical, without any emotion.

She's never been an ardent woman. She doesn't see herself that way. At least, not when she compares herself to women in movies and novels. Or even to Teresa. She's never felt that irrepressible desire her sister-in-law talks about, that impetuous passion that inflames her at all hours. She's enjoyed sex, but it's never had a leading role in her life. Not even at the beginning with Luis. He was the insatiable one. She tried to satisfy him as best she could, and it wasn't always pleasurable. Or not in the way it should have been. Because she needed time. And the pressure, another person's desire imposing itself, made her close up. Her own desire came only when it wanted to, when she least expected. More than once, she had cursed it.

One day, she caught Luis masturbating in the bedroom. They were embarrassed at first, but they talked about it, it was natural. They even made a deal: if he needed it and she wasn't in the mood, he could take care of himself and she wouldn't mind. She stopped walking into the bedroom, like a mother trying not to burst in on her teenage son. She said it didn't bother her to know her husband was masturbating in the next room over, but secretly she couldn't help but feel disappointed, knowing that she and pleasure inhabited different worlds.

Their bodies drifted slowly apart. Iván's birth, and especially her father moving in, snuffed out the last embers of passion. They only did it a few times after that, but she does remember one time that was happy, on one of those days when arousal overtakes you and yours joins another's in synchrony. That's how her desire's always been, capricious. Rarely there when she needs it.

Since Luis's death, it's stayed hidden, among other things because that was the day her body began to change. She took that as another chapter in her mourning. The organism mutating, the sleepless nights, the hot flashes, the sheets soaked with sweat, and worst of all, the feeling that her body needed constant attention, that it was more an obstacle than a tool. It wasn't a trauma for her, that transformation. In some way, it was freeing. She left behind part of herself with it. Or so she thought at first. She'd read that would happen, others had told her it would. But her body didn't disappear. She felt it more than before, as though her entrails were erupting outward. She noticed it especially on her skin, which was thinner, more transparent, more sensitive to the slightest touch. It was her mind more than her body that sent her desire into exile. Later, when she got gooseflesh—because of the feel of her sheets, or a scene in a movie or a novel, or even the wind—she's tried to restrain it with all her might, as though mourning implied the refusal of pleasure.

But tonight, she lets it loose, allows her body to find its place, frees what has been locked away for so many years. When she finishes, she feels guilty, the way she did when she touched herself as a teenager, for breaking an unspoken pact with memory. Releasing this body voluntarily bound.

The feeling lasts a few seconds. Then she falls asleep. She dreams a pair of hands is holding her in bed and pushing her into the mattress. She wakes with a start and struggles to close her eyes again. The absence at the foot of the bed is dense and threatening today. She can almost glimpse its outlines in the darkness.

2

HOW COULD SOMETHING AS INSIGNIFICANT AS a kiss have stirred her like this? She can't get Alfonso out of her mind. But it's not really him, it's the feeling: of being wanted, seen, alive. She realizes this as she gets up, looks in the mirror, and catches sight of the woman beneath the armor. She's still there, along with everything else that anchors her in the past, the strange aftertaste of guilt, the absence swallowing her, the darkness pouncing, sending echoes over everything in its path.

That same tension between two worlds attempting to exist invades her on her morning walk through the village. She's always thought two realities inhabited that place at once. Since her childhood. Often she can even see it: the real village and the fictional one, superimposed on each other. The businesses closed in winter, the ice cream shops, the bars on the boulevard, the stores along the beach...the village crouched and waiting for the heat to come. Hibernating, unseen to all but its inhabitants. Closed but waiting, empty houses, shuttered blinds, other places vanished forever.

The flood has woven together those superimposed spaces. More than a month has passed, but the vestiges are still there. Traces of water and mud, shut doors, brick walls slumping, less waiting for summer than fearing another deluge.

The distance between those two villages is gone, she thinks, the catastrophe has merged them and thrown phantasmagoric shadows across them. She feels this intensely as she walks along the boardwalk. In autumn, it's empty at this hour of the day, and cold, and she likes it that way, without tourists, it's hers, the sea's calm and the chilly breeze grazes her skin. But that solitary space no longer seems to be waiting, instead it's a relic of disaster, of a flood, and a reminder of the menace of uncertainty. Latent, invisible, and on that day in particular, she recognizes it as her own.

She feels the urge to photograph this past made present. And the daguerreotype might be the ideal medium to portray those times in conflict, which slow everything down, and the strange sense that walking through the village is a way of taking history on one's shoulders. The memory of destruction, stranded in time.

She suggests this to Clemente when she visits him the next day. And she tells him he should come with her.

She likes the solitude and concentration before taking a photograph, the pure vanishment of the self into the self and the singular dilation of time that occurs when you peer through the viewfinder. But she's not sure she's mastered the technique, and perhaps, without the old man's help, she'll botch it.

"If my body can take it," he responds. "I'm getting worse by the day. But sure, I'm there for you."

His mood throughout is contained, dry, distant. She assumes she knows what's happening, but can't figure out how to bring it up. At last, he speaks:

"That friend of yours…"

"I'm sorry if he made you uncomfortable," she interrupts him.

"He wrote the prologue to every one of those books. Is there no one else in Murcia who knows how to write?"

Dolores doesn't know what to say.

"He's pretentious, smug," Clemente goes on, standing and pointing around the room at his pictures. "Why would I give him all this?"

"It was just a proposition." She tries to calm him down.

He coughs, sits again in his chair, almost stumbles.

"See? My body's giving out on me. And then this snake in the grass comes around. He ruined my week."

She's never seen him like this. And she doesn't know if it's just his displeasure at Alfonso's intentions or something else. She doesn't think he's jealous, but she doesn't dismiss the possibility either.

"I don't know why you ever brought me up to him."

"I'm sorry, I really am."

"Now we've got to figure out how to get rid of him."

"Don't worry," she says. "I'll tell him you thought it over, and for now, the answer's no."

"Not *for now*," he says emphatically. "*Jamais!*"

"My intentions were good," Dolores says, herself a bit discomfited.

"These photos keep me company. Even if I don't see them. They're a part of me. And the collection's not done, is it? We're still taking photos. And you will go on contributing to it."

His voice has changed as he utters these last words. His body, his face relax, and his anger vanishes.

Later, he tells her he'll ready the equipment and insert the plates, and they can photograph the village any day they choose. Or that she chooses, rather. He has all the time in the world.

"I'll pay for the plates," Dolores says.

"Consider them a donation from the collection," he says sarcastically.

3

THEY LEAVE EARLY TO TAKE DAGUERREOTYPES
in the village, pleased that the light's playing along.
They've waited for a fine day like this. The autumn's
been strange. The rain hardly lets up. Water seems to
fall endlessly from the sky. But for today, at least, not a
single cloud crowds the dawn sky.

Dolores drives through the village streets. Clemente's only seen the flood's effects on TV.

"It looks like a war zone."

"Just wait," she says as they pass by the square in front
of the church, with its upturned flagstones and shattered
sidewalks. "Look here, you'd think a bomb exploded."

She's prepared four plates for the four frames Clemente has. She already has the images in mind: the
flooded ravine, with the mud streaking the canebrakes,
still untended; the cobblestoned street with the tourist
shops, all closed down, as in a no-man's-land; and the
sea, from two angles: the marina and the beach.

She likes how he looks at it all, how he lets her work, how he's sparing with his recommendations: just a few technical details to keep her from making a mistake. It's a virtue, knowing how to teach without elevating yourself above your pupil.

"The sea's always been hard to capture," he says as they walk away from the esplanade. "It never stops moving."

"This one's different. In that, too, it resembles a dead body. As opposed to…" She hesitates. "An unquiet one."

She regrets saying this as soon as it's left her lips. She imagines what Clemente would think if he knew she'd told the story to Alfonso, let alone scanned the photo from the book and emailed it to him.

He looks at her without saying a word. It's for the best, she thinks, as she prepares the bellows camera and places it on the metal tripod. In her backpack, the plates are already in their frames. She doesn't need him there, she can take care of herself, and today, because he's brought a cane with him to walk more steadily, she doesn't want him to help her carry anything.

He says he's tired, but he wants to walk toward the sea, to feel the sand of the shore beneath his feet. Noticing there's no one nearby, she leaves the camera and the equipment on a bench. She takes his arm and helps him down the stairs to the sand. When they arrive, she stops, but he says they should go on until they're closer to the water. But the sand slows him, and halfway there, he stops, stands still, and breaks the silence:

"That's fine. This was enough."

Dolores sees the satisfaction on his face from the corner of her eye. They turn around and walk back slowly. Climbing is harder than descending, and when they're finally back on the esplanade, Clemente sits on the bench where the camera and the equipment repose and lets a long groan escape him. She offers him a bottle of water from her backpack. He takes small sips and opens his mouth wide to catch his breath. Then he pounds his feet on the ground to knock the sand off his shoes and sighs.

"That was some marathon," he finally gets out. "But don't you stay here. You've still got another photo to take."

"Are you sure you're all right here?"

"I've never been better."

She picks up the camera, the tripod, and her backpack, and walks down to the beach, still thinking of Clemente. Of his hoarse breathing, but also his strange satisfaction. For a moment, she perceives some kind of leave-taking in his determination to tread the sand and approach the sea.

She mounts the camera near the shore, takes off her shoes, and walks over to the water. The dead fish are gone. The sea looks normal. But when she sinks her feet in the water, it's black. She'd read about that in the papers, but she hadn't seen it with her own eyes. The mud, the dead algae. The sea rotting. Its ordinariness is superficial, an illusion. The ruin is there, silent, crouching under the still surface.

Her memory stirs like the disturbed waters. The glassy sea of her childhood is a swamp. It even smells bad. Like a rotting body.

She attempts to capture that aspect of it, somber, ghostly, death stalking closely behind. And though she isn't sure how, something of that does show up in the daguerreotype, as she discovers later at Clemente's house, when they develop it. Of the four, it is the one that shows most palpably the phantasmagoria, the banishment from time, and the sea itself, invoking something imperceptible to the human eye. A grim wind come from the future. The invisible. Things whose existence she has always denied.

In that stillness, in that calm sea, something sinister is throbbing. Maybe it's just her own eyes, conferring meaning and history on what she sees. But Clemente detects it clearly.

"What desolation!"

That's the word, Dolores thinks. *Desolation.* Clemente is panting, weak, as he pronounces it.

"Are you all right?" she asks him again.

"A little tired, a little dizzy, but I'm pleased."

Dolores walks him from the shack back into the main part of the house. She feels his body's weight, the pressure of his fingers on her arm. He seems exhausted as he takes his seat.

At least Vasil's home today. He brings him a glass of water and puts a blood pressure cuff on his wrist. One eighty over one ten, a little high. He also slips a device for measuring oxygen saturation on the tip of his index finger.

"We've got everything you could ask for here," jokes Clemente. He never stops smiling.

"Eighty-six percent," Vasil says. "Too low."

"It's fine. It'll go back up."

"We'll call an ambulance."

Clemente's against it, but she won't be swayed. Over the phone, she explains the situation.

"They're on their way," she says when she hangs up.

Dolores doesn't leave until they arrive. It's nothing serious, the doctor says, putting a lorazepam under Clemente's tongue. His oxygen's low, he needs to go to his doctor and see about his blood pressure. He should avoid overexertion.

"You can leave, really," the old man tells Dolores when they're by themselves. "Vasil will stay with me. I'm fine."

"Are you sure?"

"I'm sure."

She hesitates. In her mind, she's responsible for him. She's the one who took him to the village. It's her fault he wore himself out.

She tells him goodbye, and in the doorway, before departing, says to Vasil, "He can't be alone."

"I'll stay with him."

"I mean..." She pauses. "His son. His son should know how his father is."

"He doesn't want family to know nothing. Family don't want him either. Like he don't exist."

Dolores wonders if he knows how to get in touch with the son, regardless of Clemente's wishes. A phone number, something. Vasil shakes his head.

"It's important," Dolores insists. And she tells him to look around the house. He must be able to find something.

Vasil's expression is irritable, as if he's been saddled with an unexpected responsibility.

The next day, Vasil calls at midmorning. He didn't find the son's number, but he has his address. Dolores thanks him for doing it so quickly. She wants to write a letter to him and explain the situation. But she wishes there were a faster way. She calls Iván and asks him if they can somehow use that address to find a phone number or some other connection.

"No luck on the email or phone number," he tells her, calling back, "but looking around on Facebook, I found an Eric Artés who lives in a little town close to

Marseille. There can't be many people there with that name."

Iván sends her a link. When she clicks on it, the Facebook app opens. Eric Artés. She can't tell anything from the photo. Just a vague figure in front of a landscape. She tries to remember how to look for more pictures. Iván opened the account for her and installed the app on her phone, but she never uses it and has almost forgotten how it works. It takes her a long time to notice the photos tab and click on it.

She examines the publicly available images. Some of them show his face. He must be more or less her age. He looks like Clemente. The same narrow eyes. The salt-and-pepper beard, the elegant bearing, even in the less formal pictures of him traveling with his family. A wife and two kids, as Clemente said. It must be him.

Dolores examines each image. His wife looks French. Her face hard, sharp, like a famous actress. Isabelle Huppert, maybe. The teenage daughters look like they've stepped out of a movie too. Always smiling, with studied poses.

Dolores feels like an intruder, peeking into a world she's not supposed to see. She's witnessing a perfect life with no room in it for Clemente. And she's not sure whether to send a message and interrupt this happy life. She goes to bed without doing so, but she can't stop thinking about it. At midnight, she gets up and turns on her phone. The light from the screen blinds her. Eyes half-shut, she opens Facebook and looks for Eric's pro-file. She writes him a concise message:

Dear Eric, I hope this message doesn't bother you. I'd like to talk to you about your father's health. Thanks, and best wishes.

4

NO ONE ELSE IS WITH THEM IN THE REFRIGER-
ated chamber. The family decided to wait outside. Alfonso's holding the reflector. Dolores tells him to move
it a little closer to the face of the deceased.

She notices his curiosity as he stares at the corpse's
purplish face. The drowned have a peculiar look, Clemente had warned her over the phone. Not even makeup
can cover the swelling and the violet shade of the skin.
She tries to ignore it and focus on her work. She should
have come alone. She'd have been more comfortable.

Last night, when Clemente phoned her to tell her he
was unwell and asked her to take this job, she thought it
would be best to go accompanied, and Alfonso seemed
like the person to ask. But this morning, she realizes
there are times when it's better to be alone. Not that she
doesn't respect him: Alfonso's working meticulously. It's
his expression, something intangible but clearly present.
Now she knows what Clemente wanted to tell her. That
it's not just arranging the camera, focusing, framing;

there's also a gaze, an attitude, something given off as one sees. Affection or morbid curiosity. She thinks she sees the latter in Alfonso. In him, the act of observation is indiscreet.

She remembers her first time. And the others too. She always tried not to look head-on, to treat the deceased person not as an inert object, but as a subject, one who might open his eyes at any moment and look back at her. The body, she thinks, isn't just what you see, it's also what can see you.

She doesn't intend to stay long, but she takes more time than needed to finish shooting. She can't afford any mistakes. She suppresses her discomfort, trains her gaze on the corpse, and continues with the ritual. Time stopped, care, attention to detail. It's the last image. It deserves all the conscientiousness she can muster. Nothing is more important than what's happening here and now.

On the way out, she'd rather not speak. But Alfonso can't wait to get to the car before showering her with enthusiasm.

"Fascinating! What aplomb! You're really something, Dolores!"

"It's called respect."

"I guess you can get used to anything."

"I hope I don't ever get used to this."

She opens the trunk of the Corsa, and she and Alfonso put everything inside. She thanks him for the help and for getting up early.

"I'm going to get the culture editor of *La Verdad* to interview you," he says. "She's a friend. I've got to tell her about this."

"I don't know…" Dolores says.

"I'll just bring it up to her, and you can decide."

"It sounds like a bad idea."

"You'll change your mind."

Dolores shakes her head and frowns. How would Clemente react? Alfonso presses her:

"Trust me. And another thing: my friend from Madrid called. About the photo of the so-called unquiet one. The word he used was *exceptional*. If it's real, it would be a true find. But it might just be a double exposure or the camera moving. We need more info. Where he got it, what its provenance is…"

"He said he lost it."

"He can tell us more than that, can't he? The guy likes you, after all."

"I don't think this is the time. He's sick."

"It matters. You should take advantage before he dies on us."

Dolores stares at him without a word. He realizes his remark was untoward and changes tack, coming closer and placing his hands on her shoulders.

"You'll find the right time."

He hugs her goodbye, rashly, not letting her go for several seconds. He doesn't kiss her. But she quivers when she feels his chest on hers. Arousal—it comes on quickly, and she can't suppress it. Despite everything. Her body awakens. The affirmation of life in the vicinity of death.

5

CLEMENTE'S FACE HAS TRANSFORMED. SPRAWLED
in his armchair, with a cannula shooting oxygen up his
nose, he seems to have aged several years in an instant.
The irritating noise of the machine has destroyed the
serenity of the house.

"I'm fine. This is just what I needed, this snorkel
going up my nose," he says, touching the thin plastic
tubes connected to the tank.

He's supposed to use the machine several hours a
day. And at night. Vasil shows her the doctor's orders, as
if she were his daughter.

"He can't be alone now," he remarks.

And he tells her Clemente has to hire someone else
for the nighttime. They thought about his wife, but she
can't keep her job at the supermarket and do this too.
Vasil can't stay there every night. He could work more
hours, sure. Stay a night or two, but not all the time.
So for now, a friend of his wife's who was unemployed
is coming from nine at night until nine in the morning.

As Vasil speaks, Dolores is tempted to say she'll help. She could stay over a few times a week too. If he needed it, she could do it. She could offer. She almost does. But at the last minute, she stops herself.

"Have you thought about moving to a facility?" she asks Clemente.

"I don't want to leave here. I want to be in my home until the end. It's my haven. But let's not talk about this, I've had enough of it for today. Show me the proofs!"

Dolores takes out the folder with the photos from her most recent job and shows them to him. She doesn't tell him Alfonso came along. He looks at them attentively for a few moments, nodding and pursing his lips. His expression is made more solemn by the small plastic tubes in the center of his face.

"You don't need me anymore at all."

"Don't say that."

"I've got a disciple," he says, looking at Vasil. Dolores sees the dampness in his eyes. Still looking, he continues, "Every day, I'm more pleased that I called her. I'm even happy I fell. Though it might cost me my life."

"Don't say that," Dolores says again.

"I don't have much left."

He's especially sensitive today. Despite this, she mentions his son as gingerly as possible. She doesn't tell him she's written him, just that he should call him and let him know how he is, have him come, keep him apprised of the situation.

"Some families don't get along," he says. "And that's all there is to say."

Dolores can't stop thinking of the pictures on Facebook, his son's apparently happy life, his daughter-in-law, his grandchildren all grown up…

"Don't you miss him? How long has it been since you saw your granddaughters? Wouldn't you like to hold them?"

"It's too late, Dolores. Let it go."

She stops insisting and says no more.

She realizes it's not the time to ask about the photo in the book. Nor does she find the mystery that intriguing. She's been thinking it over lately. She should never have brought it up. Not the unquiet ones, not the photo, not the collection. Nothing. She's imprudent sometimes, thoughtless. It's funny that she should spill others' secrets and guard so jealously her own. There are things she doesn't know how to keep inside and others she could never let out.

No, she won't ask Clemente about the photo. Not today. In his state, he doesn't need more headaches. All he needs is to have his family near him. His son, his granddaughters. That's all.

She leaves, convinced, but first opens the Facebook app on her phone and looks at the message she sent Eric. It's still there, unread, stranded in digital space.

6

TERESA IS THE FIRST ONE TO PHONE.

"You're famous. You look so good in the photo. Like a model."

"Don't tell me more," Dolores responds. "I'm going to go buy the paper right now."

She hangs up, throws on some clothes, and hurries off to the village kiosk. The forecast called for rain, but the sun's high in the sky, and it doesn't look like a single drop will fall. After buying the paper, she sits on the patio at the pastry shop by the park to read the interview. You can still see damage from the flooding: bricks fallen in the corners, bent and downed trees, mud, and puddles that will never dry.

She orders a café con leche and a croissant and flips the pages slowly, stopping on every news item before the culture pages, slowing down, postponing, drawing out the inevitable.

"Death doesn't frighten me." Dolores Ayala, photographer of the deceased. The headline runs across two pages, above

a photo of her in the shadows, a camera around her neck, leaning on the counter in her studio.

Included are two mortuary photographs from the nineteenth century. A dead man lying on a sofa and a woman with her departed son in her arms. The journalist chose the most upsetting ones to illustrate "the macabre custom of photographing the dead."

No matter what you say, they take you where they want. Teresa told her so. Working for the government, she has more experience dealing with the press. Dolores had thought she could handle the journalist. Avoid sensationalism. That's what she's learned to do in those months, view it all as natural. What's more normal, more inevitable than death? The anomalous thing, the terrifying thing, is trying to suppress it, hide it, pretend it doesn't exist. Mortuary photography presents humankind with the one certainty it possesses: its expiry. It's a keepsake of the last moment, an attempt to trap the impression of the body before it vanishes. An act of love that only appears morbid because of the nature of the contemporary gaze.

She tried to explain this to the journalist who visited her studio while they chatted amiably, coffee in hand. She showed her the contact sheets and the proofs of some of the photos she took with Clemente. But she refused to send copies via email, and now she's glad. They're privileged documents, she said.

She was happy with the conversation. She even felt a kind of strange euphoria all through the day. It was the first time she'd ever been interviewed. She's always preferred anonymity, but she found a secret satisfaction in talking publicly. She remembered when they used to interview Luis when he exhibited his works about the village. He wasn't an artist, he always tried to stress that, but he didn't dislike surrounding himself with an aura of mystery when he posed, in black, with his camera, his eyes lost in the horizon. He'd utter some severe affirmation, a sentence about life and photography, and inevitably they'd give it pride of place in the newspaper. She never minded not appearing in the photos or the text, even when the two of them had created the works together. She was his assistant. That's how she saw herself. And she preferred playing second fiddle. She was more comfortable that way.

Now she's the protagonist. But when she reaches the culture pages and sees what the interview has become, what should have been pride becomes disappointment.

She pays for breakfast and returns home with the newspaper folded under her arm. On her way, she worries about how Clemente will take it. That's the first thing that came into her head when she opened the article. Fortunately she refused to give his name. *The mysterious old man* who returned from France to photograph the dead. Hopefully he won't find out about it. But that's unlikely. And when she sees his number on her phone's screen, she fears the worst.

"You saw it?" she asks before saying hello.

"Yes. You're very photogenic. More so than the dead people."

Dolores tells him how disgusted she is with what's happened, that she tried to offer a less gruesome perspective on the tradition.

"Don't worry, the press always takes you where they want." The same phrase she heard from Teresa.

"I hope it doesn't affect our customers."

"No one reads anything," the old man consoles her. "And people forget everything right away. So don't be all glum. Especially since you look so pretty in your photo. Imagine if they took one of me. That really would be gruesome."

"Oh, you!"

She thanks him for the words of encouragement and asks him how he is.

"Fine, fine," he responds, "but I can't get used to the oxygen. And the pills they sent me sap my strength. But now that I'm a *mysterious old man*, I can die in peace."

"I'll come see you soon."

"Enjoy your fame. You're a worthy heir."

7

ALFONSO TAKES A BIT LONGER TO CALL HER, but still does before the morning's over. He thinks the interview's fine and doesn't understand why Dolores is angry. His friend's a good journalist, and she captured her subject's essence.

"Tonight, I'm paying for dinner," he says. "I'm responsible for the damages."

She didn't remember that they'd agreed to meet that day, but Alfonso insists, and she winds up folding.

"I'm just not much in the mood."

"We've got a reservation in the best place," he says. "If the problem is driving back home alone, you can stay with me. In the guest room, of course."

Before departing for the capital, Dolores looks at herself in the mirror. She doesn't expect anything to happen that night—she doesn't know if she wants anything to happen any night, at least with Alfonso. But she knows the possibility's there. As she shaves her armpits in the bathroom, a contradictory feeling possesses her, pitting her body against her mind. Not the way it used to happen with Luis, her mind wanting and her body not responding, or her mind wanting to want, even if deep down it really didn't. This afternoon's different. There's a tingle in her body. She can feel this clearly as she rubs herself down with lotion and looks in the mirror.

She doesn't dislike what she sees. She's happy with her body, its full shapes, its roundness. A Valkyrie, Luis used to call her. "It is what it is," she would respond while he gawked at her firm breasts and told her they looked like those of a Greek statue. They no longer have that firmness of marble, the curves are sagging a bit, but she still thinks they're nice. And they're still hers.

Getting old isn't the worst of her worries. It never has been. Not on the outside, at least. Wrinkles, flaccid flesh, stretch marks, spots on her face and hands...she has all these, her skin's withering, but she hasn't thought about all that for a long time. What worries her is what can't be seen, the invisible body's decline, the pain it spawns before the very end.

She looks at herself a bit longer today. But not too long. As if she doesn't want her beauty to awaken, as if she preferred to let it sleep, hide, remain out of the light. When she was a girl, compliments embarrassed her. She's never known how to act when someone praises her virtues, like Clemente when he mentioned her photo in the newspaper this morning. She's always tried not to emphasize her charms, avoiding low-cut or tight-waisted dresses. Even today, the one she picks is dark and baggy, camouflage, an armor to defend her against others' stares. As she thinks about this, she recognizes it's a way of disappearing, like the hidden mothers in the pictures. She's often told herself this is discretion, but it's also a sort of fear, a phobia of entering others' visual field, of being a body, exposed and vulnerable. She feels it invading her now, and wishes it wouldn't, but it's too late. She'll try to overcome it, to stop disappearing. Before leaving her bedroom, she adjusts her belt. Not much, just enough to show off her bust and hips, and for a moment, her body appears in all its glory in the mirror.

On the way to the city, as the first drops of rain strike the windshield, she can't stop thinking about what she's doing.

"Be happy, woman," Teresa told her yesterday. "Your body's aging, that doesn't mean it's time to suffocate it. If you don't like it, just go home. End of story."

Your body's aging, that doesn't mean it's time to suffocate it. Tonight, then, she'll try to let it breathe. She knows there's a place inside her the air can't get to, a cavity that refuses to be occupied, however much she tries to fill her lungs.

She takes a deep breath and tries to leap over the invisible barrier. She doesn't knock it down, but it budges. She's gained ground inside herself. Enough to push everything else aside and focus on the present. Saturday night, a good restaurant, an attentive man, a return to life.

The wine helps a lot. She realizes this not long after dinner starts.

"To the hot photographer of the moment!" Alfonso raises his glass.

Dolores can sense his euphoria. He sputters, making excuses for his journalist friend and saying it's normal for an interviewee to feel betrayed.

"You can't imagine the number of times it's happened to me. There's always such a distance between what you say and what appears in the article. And you're the only one who knows. The sad thing for me is that your own photos aren't featured. I still dream about that morning when I went with you."

"I don't think the families would have liked seeing their dead exposed that way."

"Sure, I get that," Alfonso corrects himself. "Years will need to pass. Until no one remembers them. Or until your photos make it into the archive."

Dolores smiles.

"By the way, how's the maestro? Is he better?"

"He's still pretty frail."

"Do we know anything more about the...photo of the unquiet one?"

"He doesn't remember anything else," she lies. "It seems to be lost."

"My friend's going to be disappointed..."

"You can tell him I appreciate his interest and his willingness to help," she interrupts him, "but honestly, he can drop it. It's better that way."

"I guess he didn't say anything about the collection either?"

She shakes her head and has a bit more wine.

"We've got to convince him, by hook or by crook. It's important we try to close the deal before the year's end. My boss is getting antsy. This would be a coup for the archive. I'd do anything to get my hands on it." He looks at her sternly and says, "Dolores, please, try to get him to listen to reason. Just try."

"I don't think this is a good time for him."

"Still? Are we going to have to wait till he's the one in the coffin to ask?"

"Don't say that."

"Come on, it's a joke."

Dolores furrows her brow and pouts. She isn't enjoying the conversation, or the remarks, or the pressure Alfonso's putting on her. She can almost see herself, her uncomfortable frown, the same grumpy face she made in pictures when she was a girl. Alfonso realizes this and changes the subject.

"You look really good today." He's eased back. "You looked good in the photo too. I'd have thought you were thirty."

Dolores thanks him for the compliment. And yet her body seems to reject it. The chair is agonizing, she keeps shifting trying to find the right position, but can't. Her back's getting stiff and she feels a pinch between her shoulders. She tries not to make a show of it and utters a few kind words to him in turn.

Alfonso really does look younger than he is. And he knows it. That tight shirt gripping his body shows that he knows it. No one wears something like that if they don't want people to look. Then there's his way of moving, his strut, as if he wants to show off what he's achieved, how he's winning the battle over age, even if sooner or later he'll have to capitulate. She imagines the hours he spends in the gym, the attention he lavishes on himself. Again, she remembers Luis. Unlike Alfonso, he threw in the towel early. He'd never taken great care of himself, and toward the end, he seemed to stop caring at all. He put on pounds, his face got fatter, he had the second chin, the belly, the flabby skin. But he never lifted a finger to do anything about it. She never chastised him. Nor did he say anything if she put on weight, or stopped dyeing her hair, or quit dressing up the way she used to. *I like you the same no matter what*, he used to say. And she liked him too. The built guy with the long hair and beard she fell in love with and the ever-tubbier guy with ever-thinner hair who was starting to get old. She never let appearances sway her. Or so she's always said, even if her desire died out over time, despite whatever traces of the body she used to lust after remained in what that body became. That's just what happens when people let themselves go.

Alfonso hasn't let himself go. Dolores imagines how hard he's struggled against the inevitable. It's commendable. She gave up a long time ago.

"You've got to try and hold on to it until you just can't anymore," he concludes and serves her a bit more wine. She's starting to feel woozy, but the buzz makes everything happier, more pleasurable. If she could only feel like that forever, if only that sensation wouldn't expire…

Outside the restaurant, it's raining. Alfonso didn't bring an umbrella. She did, she's always thinking ahead. She opens it and covers them both.

"You're not going home in this," he asserts.

"Don't worry, it's fine."

"Absolutely not. You're coming to my place. At least until it lets up. I'm close by."

"OK," she concedes. "But only if your couch is comfortable. My back's killing me."

"It's as comfortable as they come."

They walk arm in arm, strategically, to keep from getting wet. For those few minutes, Dolores is happy.

She can feel Alfonso's body, his strong hands, his hard muscles, his shapely arms.

When they reach his apartment, she asks where the bathroom is. The rain always makes her want to piss. And she's had a lot of wine, and a lot of water too. She needs a few minutes to think the situation over. What is she doing exactly? Does she know what it implies, coming up to his home after dinner? She hasn't done something like this in centuries, but she's not naïve. She's aware of what can happen. What she wants most of all is to sit on the couch and give her back a rest.

When she emerges, Alfonso's waiting in the living room. He's changed into another shirt, which he's still buttoning up.

"I was soaked. If you like, I can give you something to wear."

"I'm fine. The umbrella kept me covered."

Alfonso asks if she wants a drink. She says she prefers an herbal tea.

"Nose around as much as you like," he says. "I'll get everything ready in the kitchen."

Dolores lies back on the sofa and feels her bones settling into place as she looks around her. The coffee table is big, with a glass top; the chairs are metal, with white backing; an arc lamp shines over the leather sofa with red cushions; the rug is soft under her feet... Everything is thought-out, calculated, drawn from a home-décor magazine. She's comfortable. The apartment's got the perfect amount of warmth. And the perfect temperature, and the perfect lighting.

She looks at the paintings and photographs. One corner resembles a museum.

"It's like an exhibition hall, right?" Alfonso says, setting down a tray with the herbal tea, a bottle of whiskey, and two glasses with ice. "Most of these pieces are gifts. Or payment for texts I wrote for catalogues."

Dolores is surprised to find there some of the photos she's seen in the archive's publications.

"They're better off here," Alfonso says. "I consider them a loan. This is the best one, I think." He points to the wall farthest from the sofa.

Dolores gets up to look closely. It's a large black-and-white landscape that reminds her of a Romantic painting. An aerial view of high mountains covered with clouds. For a few seconds, she's bewitched. The sublime power of nature in all its splendor.

"It's beautiful," she says.

"It's from Sebastião Salgado's most recent exhibition. The regional government purchased it. And then it wound up in the office of some minister who didn't appreciate it. It's better off here."

"Is that legal?"

"Believe me, it's better off here."

Dolores doesn't ask again. She returns to the sofa, and when she sits down, she can't help sighing with pleasure. She knows it sounds like something else though.

"Sorry. It's just those restaurant chairs are so uncomfortable."

Alfonso sits down next to her.

"You can moan all you want. Far be it from me to tell you to pipe down."

She smiles. She's tired and nervous. He takes her hand, caresses it, and brings it to his lips. She sighs again, softer, it sounds almost like an echo. They look at each other. They're close. Alfonso pulls her to him and kisses her. She feels his tongue, rough, with a metallic flavor of alcohol. She lets herself go and relaxes her lips.

Alfonso slides his arms down her back. Again, this is a first. She's not ready. But her body is. At least for now. She grabs him and hugs him tight, kisses him, wraps her tongue slowly around his. But when he reaches under her dress and his hands rest on her thighs, her body shuts down, ceases moving along. Alfonso shows no intention of stopping. It is, subtly, a battle: two bodies in combat.

Alfonso's hands grab her buttocks. His fingers sink into her flesh. She leans back slightly, trying to escape.

"Sorry," she manages to say.

"Don't you like it?"

"Yeah...but I'd rather..."

"Relax," he whispers. "It's fine."

And he comes in again, and his hands grip her buttocks, caress her thighs. She bears it a while longer, glances down, notices his erection. He's proud of it, his pants about to explode. He pulls her into him, trying to make her feel his hardness. Dolores looks away, pulls back. He strokes it and pulls it down, so it sticks out even farther.

When he touches her thighs again, she feels his hands rising, trying desperately to get at her sex. She imagines them like two serpents creeping up her body toward their prey. They get past her leggings and smoothly reach inside, caressing her lace panties.

She hears him groan, his hand under the seams, stroking her pubis. She wants to accept it, tries to make her body go along, in violation of herself. But her body resists, struggles, for Dolores this isn't a game, it hasn't been for some time now. When she feels Alfonso's fingers inside her, she grabs his hand hard and stands up abruptly.

"I'm sorry," she manages to say. "I can't. I need to go."

"What?" His expression is somewhere between incredulity and rage.

"Sorry, I really am, but I'm leaving."

"I don't understand."

"Sorry."

She can't think of anything else to say. She repeats it in the mirror in the elevator, patting down her dress and trying to regain composure before walking outside. She murmurs it between clenched teeth as she walks, jogs almost, under the rain to her car, soaking her shoes.

She says it as she's driving home, in the small hours of morning, almost unable to see the road, rain thrashing the windshield, water flowing in sheets across the road. I'm sorry. But what is she sorry for? Who's she saying this to? To Alfonso, who pulled himself together and accompanied her to the door in silence? Herself, because she took her own body to its limit? Luis, whom she can't get out of her head, no matter how hard she tries? To none of them and all of them at the same time.

All she wants right now is to get home fast. It was foolish to go to his apartment. It was foolish to leave and drive off in these conditions too. Alfonso wasn't going to rape her. At least, she thinks he wasn't. Even if he didn't stop when she obviously wanted him to. She also didn't make him. She was struggling against herself as well as him.

Either way, it's not the time to clarify her thoughts.

The road requires all her attention.

The rain is falling harder. The alcohol is still clouding her head. She could have called Iván, but she didn't want to bother him. She could have looked for a hotel and waited out the storm. But that night, she just wants to get home, take off her dress and heels, and stretch out in bed.

The drive takes forever, the road seems endless, the exit won't appear. When at last she veers off and sees the lights of the village, time slows down further, as if the car were stationary, or the village had moved several miles farther off.

When she gets there, she takes an ibuprofen and lies in bed, tense and exhausted. Her head hurts, her back and jaw hurt too. She's been grinding her teeth the whole way. The rain pounds the roof like an earthquake. She closes her eyes and her breathing calms. She made it. She's home. No one can harm her here.

When she turns, she feels the absence next to her. She opens her eyes and looks defiantly into the darkness. There's nothing there. A slightly darker point. She reaches out and pierces it with her hand and feels a vibration, her hair standing up on end.

"Leave me alone!" she shouts to the nothingness.

She turns back, relaxes her jaws, relaxes her body, and waits for sleep to come.

V

POISON

· · ·

1

A THUNDERBOLT WAKES HER. IT'S RAINING hard. All night, it hasn't let up. She dresses in the first thing she can find and goes to see if water's entered the studio. Everything looks all right. Just a little leaking in under the door. She grabs a towel from the bathroom, folds it up, and pushes it tight there, as she should have done last night when she arrived. Once she's dried off everything else, she takes a look in the garage. The water is nearly an inch high. But there's nothing on the floor, just the car. So she's lucky. She thinks it will stop raining soon.

She walks back upstairs to the living room and turns on the TV. "Another cold drop. Two in a span of just three months. We're talking rain on top of rain," the weatherman says jocosely, but it isn't funny.

On the news, the same images as before. The village flooded. The avenue, the restaurant in the port, the shops. The trash bins, even the cars float away like paper boats. Again, the ravine has overflowed and a river rages cruelly through the streets. She's hypnotized by the video that plays over and over while the presenter bemoans the situation. A backhoe is demolishing the wall along the boardwalk to save the houses and channel the water into the sea. With it gone, everything looks uniform: a limitless surface of brown water, carrying mud and filth, merging with the salt water of the sea. The village in the sea, the sea in the village. The village adrift.

It's still early, but she calls Iván.

"Stay home!" she orders him, just as she did a few months ago. She felt then, as she feels now, that her son is safe in the city. More than in the village, which has grown dangerous, with its buildings on the verge of collapse.

"Do you need anything?" he asks her.

"Don't worry. Just don't come here. You're better off there."

She calls Teresa too. Water's found its way into her house. Again. At least she had time to lift up her furniture and everything.

"All morning I've been bailing water. It's a disaster!"

Dolores offers her help, and Teresa thanks her. Luckily, she's not alone, she tells her. Alfonso's friend Raúl, the one she met at their dinner in the city, has been there for a few days and is giving her a hand.

"He comes to spend the weekend with me and look what happens. He's going to get tired of cleaning up all this mud."

Teresa's words calm her. At the same time, they inspire a perplexity bordering on jealousy. How quickly others put their lives back together. What skill they have at escaping solitude, finding someone to lean on. She, too, would like to have someone by her side. Someone to help her move the furniture at the house in the village—she's grateful now she put off buying anything new after the September flood—someone to help her dry the floor, someone to tell her don't worry, you're lucky, the house is fine, your son's fine, everything's fine. But there's no one to console her. So she has to say these words to herself, aloud. You were lucky. Very lucky. Last night, too, driving through the storm. If you'd waited a few more hours, the water could have carried away your car.

Now tranquil, she considers the situation and her own impulsiveness. What happened with Alfonso seems far away. Not unimportant, but far from demanding her attention. She knows, though, that she'd prefer not to hear from him a while. When a message comes through on her phone—*I hope you're all right. You should have stayed*—she responds curtly: *I'm fine. Thanks.*

The rain continues all week. The damages, once more, are beyond calculating. But the worst thing is the almost contagious sorrow in the air. It's not even rage, just the feeling that once more, everything's collapsed, Sisyphus's stone is rolling back downhill. Once more, the ravine's waters have leaked into the Mar Menor. Ruin again. Ruin atop ruin. She knows it when she goes out and feels the mud beneath her feet. The damp, the cold, the brown sludge on the streets.

She offers help to her neighbors. She and everyone else. The solitude of home dissipates outside. On the street, no one's alone. And that consoles her. A place to breathe in the midst of the melancholy. This is exactly what she needs to photograph. The neighbors, the families, the companionship. Not just the end, the ruins. Life, still throbbing, overcoming disaster.

That's what appears in the photos she takes when the rain dies and the waters abate. She feels like someone from another era, documenting the village people's strength—that community she is part of and that she feels proud of just now. Or not just now, she always has, but the feeling has grown more powerful as the week draws to an end. The blinds rise, life returns. In the restaurant in the port, the one in the square, the bookstore, the supermarket by the church. The capacity to rise up, over and over.

We'll be here, the neighbors repeat, no matter how many times we need to be here. Some will sell, some will go, some won't be able to take it anymore. But others will stay. And as long as we resist, life will go on here. Despite the uncertainty. You have to live with it. And you have to fight so it won't happen again. Dolores feels this, too, the conviction that living there means inhabiting a transitory present, ephemeral, uncertain. Being aware of the fragility of yourself and everything else.

One day, as she's out taking pictures in the village, she recognizes Clemente's friend's daughter. Ascensión, she thinks her name was. She still remembers them talking about the old man, and how the woman's words and insinuations depressed her. And she needs to speak to her urgently. But she doesn't want to interrupt her. She's holding a hose and trying to clean off the furniture from one of the restaurants on the square. Dolores observes the scene. The tables, the piles of metal chairs. The dirt resisting the pressure of the water. A small brown swamp on the ground.

She supposes Ascensión wouldn't care to appear in her work, and she waits for her to go inside before snapping this still life of destruction. When this is over and the roads have reopened, she'll visit Clemente and ask him to lend her his equipment. She wants to do it on her own now. The past few days, she's attempted to portray life. The daguerreotype captures something else: duration, time condensed but not stopped. Both are necessary, and for each object there's an appropriate technique. What she needs this week is a record of the explosiveness of an instant. She's sure of this as she develops her film and sees the gestures of support, the impetuous strength of the bodies, the way they rise up against sorrow and lighten adversity. The crush of the multitude moving onward amid catastrophe.

That same week, she opens her Facebook account over and over, awaiting a response from Clemente's son. She notices one afternoon that the icon has changed.

Read December 6.

Now she just needs him to want to write back.

2

SHE CAN TELL RIGHT AWAY THE OLD MAN ISN'T well. He's frail, his breathing's weary, his voice hoarse. His cannula is now a permanent part of his face, the oxygen machine is another piece of furniture, the house has become a hospital. Pills on the table, the glass of water, the blood pressure cuff. The clothing: the robe, the pajamas, the slippers. It's the first time she's seen him this way, even if the robe of dark silk looks like an overcoat and the gray flannel pajamas like a suit.

He answers her questions in monosyllables, contained, distant. She's gone there to see how he is, but she also wants to know when she can use the daguerreotype equipment: the camera, the fuming box, the chemicals. She's decided she wants to keep taking those pictures that condense time.

Clemente gives her the address of the workshop in Jávea where she can order plates and chemicals.

"You can use the camera and the boxes here. Everything else too."

"I wouldn't want to break anything."

"Look, I'm going to give it all to you. I doubt I'll be able to use it again."

His dry tone clashes with the generosity of his words. Dolores thanks him, but can't understand his coldness. Soon, though, she learns where it's come from.

"Why'd you have to say anything?"

"Excuse me?"

"About the unquiet ones. Your...friend was here." He pauses before the word *friend*. "And he asked me about the photo in the book."

Dolores looks at him dumbfounded.

"You didn't tell me it was a secret."

"It's not. But I said what I said in confidence."

"I'm sorry." It's the only thing she can think of to say.

"I don't want to ever hear from him again."

"I really am sorry." Saying this takes her back to what happened more than a week ago at Alfonso's. "I don't know why he came to bother you."

Clemente removes the cannula to speak and tells her Alfonso showed up without warning the day before with several books from the archive under his arm. He was there to talk about the unquiet ones, he said. An acquaintance of his was interested in the photo from the book and could look further into it. Clemente told him it was nothing, that the camera had moved during exposure and that the unquiet ones were simply a myth. An invention. Alfonso didn't press him further.

"He got around to what he was really here for," Clemente says, increasingly upset. "The goddamn collection. *Putain!* He laid a contract for donation down on this very table and asked me to sign it." He strikes the wooden surface with his fist.

"I don't know what to say. It's my fault."

"I told him to go to hell and never come back."

Enraged, Clemente starts coughing. He reaches for the glass of water on the table. Dolores brings it closer.

"He's a vulture," he continues. "Waiting for me to kick the bucket. Well he can damn well keep waiting."

She comes close to him and takes his trembling hand.

"I'm so sorry. I shouldn't have told him anything. I never imagined…"

"Some piece of work. *Connard*…"

"I…" she starts to say. "I couldn't imagine. And you told me I had a good eye…"

"For photos. You've got a good eye for photos." Finally, Clemente lets a shadow of a smile escape him. But weakly. He replaces his oxygen tubes and concentrates on trying to breathe. Dolores observes him in his enervation.

"I'm worried about you."

"Worry about making good daguerreotypes. I can take care of myself."

He calls Vasil and tells him to take her outside and help her carry the equipment to the car. As she gathers everything, she considers how valuable it all must be to him.

"It's a loan," she tells him when saying goodbye.

"It's whatever you want it to be."

Dolores thanks him. His face has softened, though the anger's still evident.

"Just one thing," he says. "Don't tell that idiot friend of yours anything else."

Dolores leaves, ashamed. She waits until she's home to call Alfonso and ask for an explanation.

"He told me you were pressuring him."

"Pressuring him, he says... I went to see how he was and I took him a few books. Obviously I asked him if he'd decided what to do. I don't want him to die and for us not to get the collection."

"What did you say about the unquiet ones?"

"Dolores, I don't know what you're talking about."

"Do you not see he's sick?"

"Crazy's what he is. He threw the books I gave him in my face and kicked me out."

"As he should have."

"As he should have?"

"You had no right to show up at his house like that."

"I don't understand."

"You even took him a contract to sign, trying to get him to donate…"

"I made him an offer we've never made in the history of the archive and the old shit tore the papers up right in front of me and almost broke my pen."

"Why don't you leave him alone?"

"You know what? The old fucker can die, as far as I care. They can bury his goddamn collection with him."

Dolores doesn't know how to respond. He continues: "You could have helped more too." Now he's showing his true colors. "All I asked you for was one thing, and you wouldn't lift a damn finger. After all I've done for you… You didn't thank me for the interview I set up, I almost had to apologize for it. And the other night, why'd you come upstairs if you didn't want anything? Can you imagine what that felt like? That's not how it works. I give you everything and you act like you always deserve more. You think you're someone. You're just a small-town girl with a camera."

Dolores can't believe what she's hearing, all the bitterness Alfonso's carrying around when they've known each other so little time. She can't bear this litany of insults any longer. She wants to scream, the way Clemente did. But she takes a breath instead and says simply:

"We're done. Bye."

She feels like telling him what she thinks about him, the other night, how he behaved with Clemente. But she doesn't. Bye. That's enough. Sometimes, she thinks, it's better to escape, evade, forget, throw off the scent. And that's what she does. Hanging up and, like a reflex, erasing his number.

She's not even hurt by what he said. She's more upset that he's bothered Clemente. That's what really gets to her.

She looks at her Facebook. It's almost a routine now. The message still shows *read*. But that isn't enough. So she writes again. *Please. It's urgent. Your father's very sick. He'd like to talk with you.*

3

A VILLAGE GIRL WITH A CAMERA, HE SAID. Maybe that's what she is. But she likes that. Sometimes an insult is only an insult to the person who utters it. For the person who receives it, it's something else. What's wrong with being a girl from the village with a camera? Luis was a guy from the village with a camera, and she was proud of that.

The studio existed partly because of his sense of vocation. The village fit into his plan. It needed pictures, and he would be the one to give them. For more than a decade, they were witness to the inhabitants' joys, their dreams, their special occasions. They captured children laughing, couples hugging, families posing, young couples seducing each other. Their photos are on the shelves and wardrobes in many local homes, monuments to their gaze. So sure, she's a village photographer. What could be more dignified than that? She wishes she had it all back, the studio the way it was, a forge for representations of the village, Luis walking through the door loaded with reels of film, her shut away for days developing happy scenes, moments that marked the memory of a generation.

It's in that inner sanctum, that holy of holies, that Dolores now stands, unpacking the material Clemente has lent her. Wood and glass boxes to expose the plates of silvered copper, the small polishing machine, the jars of chemicals, even the fuming box for the mercury vapors. She doesn't know how the images will turn out, but she's determined.

A village girl with a daguerreotype camera, she tells herself. And she smiles.

For days, she follows the same routine, getting up early and walking around looking for the perfect shot. She finds two, maybe three possible scenes. Then she goes home, prepares the plates, and returns with the camera to take her daguerreotypes.

The streets, usually silent in winter, seem somber now. The mud, the sea's biting cold. She can almost hear her steps echo.

More than ever, she's aware that the gaze takes the picture before the camera does. And it has returned to her in these months: the capacity to see, to walk between times.

It's happening as she finds herself at the old spa next to the sea. This will be one of the images. The building, from the early twentieth century, looks like an abandoned mansion. It's always filled her with a strange melancholy. She remembers it full of tourists when she was a girl, but even then, it was old and decaying. She's never stayed there, but a few years ago, after the renovations, she went with some friends of Teresa's to look at the rooms. The wooden doors painted blue, the tiles halfway up the walls, the Arabic patterns of the flooring, the picture frames, the scent of closed chambers. She doesn't know if it's because Luis had died not long before that, or if she was depressed because of her father's illness, but a wave of sorrow overtook her, as if time had stopped there, too, and not even the hordes of people in the courtyard or on the restaurant's terrace, so buoyant in those summer months, could make her feel otherwise.

The despair that filled her in those rooms is now in the very air. Despite attempts at cleaning, mud covers everything. The bright brown of filth, the color of despair.

She walks around the spa searching for the right perspective: the entrance, approaching from the beach. From there, the esplanade is visible too. Or what's left of it. The fallen granite blocks she saw on the news. She took a daguerreotype of it with Clemente. Now it's gone. At least, the way she remembered it. Those daguerreotypes are a part of history, reflecting a time that no longer coincides with the present.

She looks at the sea, choppier than usual. There's no one there. The sky's cloudy, the early December cold keeps people from going out. She struggles to find the corner where she can see the sea, with the village to one side, the wind shaking the palm trees.

She returns with her camera, inserts the plate, and leaves the lens exposed as long as she can, even at the risk of saturating the image. She's sure it will turn out badly, but she doesn't mind. She sees why later: the series of lines across the plate, the movement of the wind and water. She can't help but think of the unquiet ones. Not just because of the unsettled landscape, but also because of poison and death. That feeling overtakes her slowly, as the blurry spa comes into view, a small silhouette that won't fully take shape, a soft reflection on the surface.

Something went wrong. The exposure time or the preparation of the plate. Or maybe the quantity of mercury. She tries to pay closer attention. Rereads the steps in the instructions Clemente gave her. More than that, she thinks back over each and every one of her movements. She doesn't let it upset her. She can hear his warning in her head: there's no guarantee the subject will appear. Every time reality is imprinted on a plate, it's a miracle. And you have to look at it that way.

She polishes the plates more carefully and is exacting as she exposes them to the iodine and bromine. A bitter scent wafts through the mask and burns her eyes. She isn't worried about the saturation, she just wants to see what she saw, no matter what. She leaves the lens open a long time again. Uses more mercury, takes her time developing.

At the end of the week, she has something clearer. Not technically perfect—not like the ones Clemente developed. Any professional daguerreotypist would discard them, but for her, they're beautiful. The silhouette of the spa. The esplanade. The shifting sea. She can almost make out the volume of the mercury on the fine layer of silver that covers the plate, almost watch it travel across it, as if it were a living thing with a throbbing surface. She even thinks she hears a soft vibration, and brings it to her ear to check. But all she can be certain of is she's spent too long in the darkroom and needs to get out as soon as possible.

4

ALL WEEK, SHE HAS HEADACHES, AND AT NIGHT, mad dreams and nightmares. She attributes this to the mercury vapors, the iodine and bromine. She ought to carefully dose out the amounts and use a mask to filter the chemicals. She ought to be careful. Clemente told her so, and she's read that too. Louis Daguerre had constant headaches and felt time slow down as if he'd taken barbiturates, and he was obsessive, too, thinking the world was in decline and everything would soon end. This melancholy about his era would haunt him to the end of his days.

She's been feeling something similar in recent weeks. A dizziness, an estrangement, nostalgia for a reality that's constantly vanishing. It's more intense than usual tonight, and she struggles to get to sleep. Even when she closes her eyes, the images are still there: the ones she has seen and the ones reflected on the silvered plates. Everything is moving in her head. Her body quivers, as if folding inward, as if at its center lay a dark void that was swallowing her into the center of the bed.

It's not the first time she's experienced such a thing. She tries to remember the last time she felt it, and soon she remembers. It was a night like any other. One of Luis's friends had brought over a hash brownie, and she tried it, not knowing the secret ingredient. Her stomach started aching, she lay in bed dizzy, and her extremities shrank, her body shriveled, compressed like a collapsing star.

The memory is clear—there's a physical sensation that reminds her of that night and what happened after, which she's never forgotten. Among other things, because of the argument she had with Luis. She didn't know what she was eating while everyone sat there staring at her, and later, when they told her what was in it, she kept her composure and laughed it off. But inside, rage consumed her. She waited for everyone to leave before reproaching Luis.

"I didn't think it would bother you," he said, still laughing. "You can't tell me you didn't have fun."

The hash wore off long before her anger subsided. It wasn't that she was angry about taking drugs, it was the betrayal. Maybe that wasn't the right term, but that was how she saw it. A betrayal. She's never liked being left out of something everyone else knows. Being excluded from the conversation. Inside jokes, comments that go over her head, as if she didn't exist. She couldn't stand how everyone else was in on it. Maybe that was why she hadn't digested his absences toward the end, the feeling that he had expelled her from his life, his meetings, his friendships, his evenings out, his motorcycle rides, the whole happy world she'd never form part of, his longing to return to a time she wasn't part of.

The feeling is back. And with it, the guilt when she reminisces. It won't stay in its place, no matter what she does. The motorcycle speeding away. Her cursing him for leaving her alone.

I hope to God you crash.

She may have even said it aloud. Her last words to him, coming out of her mouth like a spell, making the accident happen.

She's never escaped this burden since: her fleeting wish, and then what happened later. This is why she was a coward. She didn't dare look Luis in the face. Not in the morgue, not at the funeral home. She couldn't make herself. That must be the origin of the absence. The one that cuts through her and is always there with her. The emptiness. The memory of what's no longer there. What she still can't dare to imagine.

She's had this foreboding for months, but hasn't really thought it through: how every last image is also the image of Luis. Every stranger's face gives detail to his absent face. Maybe that's why she's kept taking pictures lately, to try and fill in that emptiness.

This thought envelops her like a skein as the night wears on, as memories and reflections come and go. But because of the chemicals, or because of all that's been happening, the threads of the skein start to unravel. As she tries to sleep, the vapors take her to that evening she prayed so many times she'd forget. The torment. She relives it. The venomous desire. I hope you crash. I hope you choke. I hope you're miserable. The moment has swelled in her memory, spread like a virus, contaminating everything else. But at last she manages to see that wish for what it was. A mote of dust, a meaningless blot on their history together. Fleeting rage, a fleeting notion. That's all. She can't blame herself for wanting not to be left alone with her sorrow. She puts that recollection in its place, gives it the space it deserves, and feels, for the first time, the absence that accompanies her dissipating. Everything around her twists and shrinks, her body shakes and contracts from the chemicals, but still she stays firm, finding at last something to grab on to.

She doesn't forget Clemente. She calls him. He keeps getting weaker. Vasil says he's stable, but he's struggling to breathe.

The most recent call worries her: the doctors decided to send him to the hospital. He's getting less oxygen than they thought, and they need to monitor him for a few days.

When she hangs up, Dolores opens her Facebook and looks at the last message she sent Clemente's son. It says *read*. It has for more than a week.

She shouldn't get involved. No one asked her to. But she can't help writing:

Your father's in the hospital. Please, he needs to talk to you. Here's my number. It's urgent.

That same day, before bed, she notices a red alert notification on her Facebook icon. The message is concise:

Hello, Miss. I don't want to know about my father. Please stop writing me.

5

SHE THOUGHT ABOUT IT A LONG TIME BEFORE walking into the bar and asking the man working there to get her. Ascensión comes out of the kitchen and recognizes her. Of course she remembers her, the photographer, right? She tells her to wait, she'd be happy to talk to her. The bar usually empties out around ten, she should be able to take a break then.

Dolores sits at a metal table by the door and waits with a strong hot coffee in front of her. She tossed and turned all night and didn't get to sleep until just before dawn. Clemente's son's message disturbed her. *I don't want to know about my father.* What could have happened for a son to say that about the person who gave him life? Sleepless, still dizzy and lightheaded, she remembered meeting the daughter of Clemente's friend months before, and what she said in the port: *Ask him why he's all alone.* She couldn't stop thinking about it. And when she got up, not sure what she was doing, she walked to the bar where she saw her outside the other day, scrubbing off the chairs and tables.

She's still asking herself why she's there as the first sip of coffee burns her palate, and she asks for a glass of water to cool her mouth off and wash away the bitter taste. Her thoughts are a tangle as she watches Ascensión exit the kitchen and sit in front of her, unknotting her apron strings behind her with one hand.

Without preambles, almost without letting her say hello, Dolores reminds her of their conversation at the end of summer and her insinuations about Clemente.

"I knew you'd get tired of him," she says, as if she'd been waiting for her. "You seem like a sensible woman."

Dolores tells her she keeps trying to talk to Clemente about his family, but she's never gotten any answers.

"Of course you haven't. Why would he tell you about what he did?"

"What?"

"With his wife."

"What do you mean?"

"The poison."

Dolores stares at her, baffled, as she begins to talk without hesitation:

"Apparently they found several vials of poison among the medicines the poor woman was taking. The story is, she died of cancer, but I wouldn't be surprised if the sicko killed her."

Unsure how to react, Dolores twists up the unused sugar packet from her coffee. Ascensión looks toward the bar, and when she catches her coworker's eye, she points at Dolores's glass of water to ask for one herself. Then she continues, as if she were being interviewed for an exposé:

"I don't know because I wasn't there, OK. But I did see what happened when I went to the funeral with my father. I've never been more uncomfortable in my life. I felt bad for him. But remember, I didn't know what the deal was at the time. I just see an old man alone there in the corner. And on the other side are the son and the daughter-in-law and their two daughters, come over from France. They took turns going up to the glass. People didn't know who they were supposed to give their condolences to."

The bartender comes over with the glass of water and places it next to her, and she thanks him and drinks almost all of it in one sip.

"After the funeral," she continues, "they took the ashes, and they haven't been back to Spain since. That's what my father said. He said the old man was hurt and didn't like talking about it. That he swore he'd done nothing wrong. He'd just taken a photo. He said it was a misunderstanding, and now they'd stolen all he had left of his wife. I guess his son left his mother's ashes in the town she was from, in the family tomb. I heard that from one of his cousins, who talked to them before they went back to France. The same guy told me about the poison, the son mentioned it to him."

Dolores barely blinks as she listens. She imagines seeing herself from outside, face immobile, like a statue.

The other woman leans back in her chair and takes a breath:

"I know you didn't like what I said when you saw me in the port. But that man's always given me the creeps, you know? He was good to my dad, I won't deny that. They used to talk about travel, history. Dad considered him a close friend. But those photos of dead people…I always thought they were crazy. And that illness, it had to come from somewhere. I don't know if it was the picture of his wife that ruined things with him and his son, or if there was something else. But I do know what I saw at the funeral. The hatred in his son's and his daughter-in-law's eyes. The distance. You can sense that. You notice it. What could a father do to his son to make him withhold forgiveness, even at his wife's funeral? I couldn't imagine until I heard what I heard."

Dolores sips her coffee automatically. The dregs are cold, the sweetener dense in the bottom of the cup.

She finally asks, "Are you sure?"

"I'm sure of what I saw. I could put you in touch with the cousin who told me the rest if poor Manolo was still alive. Anyway, I don't know why you're getting involved."

Dolores shrugs, frowns.

"Me neither," she responds. Then she sighs and says again, "Me neither, honestly."

And she doesn't. She can't say why she's doing what she's doing. And when she tells the woman goodbye, after thanking her for her patience, this uncertainty lingers in her head, even once she's left and is nearing home. The story she heard snags inside her. She can't stop seeing the vial of poison. And her thoughts flow inevitably toward the unquiet ones.

Poison. Photography.

She tries not to let her imagination run ahead of her. But she can't help it.

6

SHE NEEDS TO TALK TO HIM, CLEAR EVERY-
thing up. She thought this when she went to bed last
night, and it kept her from sleeping. Since she talked to
Ascensión, it's been bothering her, and she's trying to
figure out how to put it in words as she drives to Santa
Lucía hospital. She still is as she gets into the elevator
and presses the button for the third floor, walks down
the hallway and looks for room 323, nudges the door,
and finds Clemente stretched out in bed in a tangle of
tubes and wires.

He looks over and purses his lips as he sees her walk
in. Resignation, she thinks. Vasil rises from the chair by
the bed and reaches for her hand.

Dolores is lost at first. All the things she thought she
might say stick in her throat. The speech she'd prepared,
the way she'd practiced to herself: I know it's gossip and
I shouldn't have paid it any attention, but I need you to
tell me, just tell me it's a lie and I don't have anything
to worry about...All those phrases want to come out,

but now she can't manage to open her mouth, can't even come up with a way to break the silence. Fortunately, Vasil does it for her:

"He's better. Doctor said so. Tired, delicate, but will get better. Just need rest."

Dolores sits down by the bed. Clemente's eyes seem to thank her for coming, or to tell her it wasn't needed. He looks abashed. Always so neat and elegant, he now has a shaggy beard, dirty, uncombed hair, badly buttoned blue pajamas...He's a different person. Not so much old as decrepit. It surprises her to think of him this way, but it's true.

The television is tuned to the local channel. The young woman in the next bed over gazes at the screen. Dolores watches for a few seconds—it's an interview show—but she can't really grasp what she's seeing. The screen is like an aquarium, something to stare at to avoid talking, or sidestep an awkward situation.

Dolores tries to hide her discomfort. Successfully, she thinks.

"Don't worry," she says, "you'll be out of here soon."

"Feet first," he murmurs. She has to get close to hear him. His voice is going.

"At least you've kept your sense of humor."

He smiles. Seeing him like this, she can't imagine he did what Ascensión said. He's a good man. She would swear that to anyone. You can see it in his face. He's always been kind to her. But for this very reason, she needs him to refute everything, to tell her none of it is true. She hesitates. The question is on the tip of her tongue. But she decides not to speak. How can she bother Clemente with rumors spread by a stranger? This isn't the time. But uncertainty has her in its grip. Misgivings have invaded her, and she can't get free of them. She has to know. She has to do something, anything, to answer this question.

Without realizing it, she tells him she'd like to take more daguerreotypes, to polish her technique, and she needs more plates. She knows he still has quite a few. Maybe she could use them. He nods and gestures to Vasil, twisting his closed fist as if turning a key in a lock.

"Key," Vasil says. "Yes, I give it to her."

Dolores stays a while, trying to pretend everything is all right. She tells Clemente about her daguerreotypes, her developing mistakes, and the few decent images she wound up with. He looks at her attentively, with interest, as if her attempt at entertaining him were the most important thing in the world.

After enough time has passed that leaving won't be rude, she looks at the clock and tells Clemente goodbye.

"I'll come see you soon," she says, resting a hand on his shoulder.

His eyes dampen. Dolores can hardly hear him say thanks.

Vasil follows her to the door, fishing a ring of keys from his pocket. Dolores nearly asks him what she'd wanted to ask Clemente, but before she can speak, he closes the door to the hallway and says:

"He's not well. Doctor says he don't hold on long like this. Oxygen not reach blood."

She wants to tell him she's written Eric and he doesn't want to see his father, but Vasil looks so upset that she decides it's best to say nothing. She pockets the keys he's taken off the ring and tells him she'll give them back soon.

"No need," he responds. "I have copy at home. Keep them. You are like daughter."

7

CLEMENTE'S AROMA GREETS HER, THAT BLEND
of wet wood and darkroom chemicals impregnating
every corner of the house. She missed that in the hospital room. The scent is so dense, it's as if he's surrounding her, and she imagines him sitting in his chair in the
living room, where Dolores stops in front of the large
daguerreotype hanging from the wall. Clemente took it
down when Alfonso visited. Now it's back in its place.
She examines it closely for several minutes, from one
side, to avoid seeing her face's reflection. She lingers
over each detail. It's perfect, crystal clear, as though en-
graved with a chisel. She couldn't say when it was taken.
Gisèle—she hasn't forgotten her name—must be around
thirty in it. The boy in her arms, maybe four or five.

Now, with what she knows, what she was told, it
looks different. Her gaze has changed. Both subjects are
far away now: Eric, the son, has another life he's trying to protect, and Gisèle, the mother, has vanished in
time and space. Dolores thinks it strange that she hasn't

seen a mortuary photo of her. She remembers the album
Clemente showed her. Gisèle wasn't in it. Or at least,
Dolores didn't notice her.

She goes to the room where he keeps his collection—
the home museum that made Alfonso so anxious. She's
never been there alone. She feels the pictures looking
back at her. The lifeless eyes of the dead, surveillance
cameras keeping watch over her privacy.

She stops thinking about them and locates the albums piled on the table, the same ones Clemente showed
her before. She has time, and is sure no one will interrupt her, but she hesitates. She's still afraid of being
caught. Finally, she sits down in the chair and begins
looking through them. She sees the old man's friends.
A directory, he called it the day he visited the shop. The
important people to him. Almost all of them men. Few
women, few young people. Incredible, the number of
people we lose in the course of a life. Love and friend-
ship mean mourning in the future. That's why some
people stop loving others, from the fear of loss. Maybe
she's one of those. Or became one these past few years.
Still thinking this, she carefully turns the pages. She
can't find Gisèle anywhere.

She opens the door to the cabinet where Clemente
keeps his *archive of failures*, and there, too, she finds
nothing: just blurry pictures, damaged ones, out of
focus, nothing like what she's looking for. But what is
she looking for? A photo of an unquiet Gisèle? Signs of

a body dying in front of the camera? She doesn't want to say. Even to think it frightens her.

What she does find is the old man's face, blurry from movement, in the daguerreotype she took not so many weeks ago. It feels like an eternity, because of what happened afterward, and also the remoteness of the moment when it was taken, and she has the impression that what she's looking at appeared on the copper plate of its own volition.

There are no other pictures of Clemente. How odd—a professional photographer with no record of his own memories. Where are the trips, the past, the memories? His family, Gisèle, Eric, his life…Where is death?

Like a detective, she keeps digging, like a spy inspecting a house in search of a hidden document or an intruder snooping around, betraying the trust a friend has placed in her. The feeling deepens when she goes upstairs and enters his room. She opens the door, and his scent envelops her more intensely, so dense it frightens her. That scent—it, too, is watching over her.

The first thing she notices is the large wardrobe in front of the bed, which resembles the ones downstairs. It's unlocked. Everything is. That eases her mind. It shows Clemente's not keeping secrets. But her guilt at invading his privacy only worsens now that she knows this.

There she finds Gisèle. Husband and wife. Son too. The family, the past. All the photos are there, ordered by year in little envelopes with their negatives. She should have expected this from someone so methodical. She breathes a bit easier.

She examines the photos from their courtship. There's a special way of looking at the camera when the photographer and the model are in love. She knows. She has many similar photos of her own. Her staring at Luis, Luis staring at her. The lens as the beloved's eye, the machine as the vehicle of warmth.

The Mar Menor. She isn't sure which beach. She thinks it's in Santiago de la Ribera. The archways of the hotel in the background are familiar, but she can't name the place. It's their honeymoon, maybe. The matte finish takes her to another time. Her childhood. Perhaps Clemente and Gisèle were among those French tourists she used to see as a girl. She lingers over the sight of the happy couple.

Then the son appears. Pregnancy, a baby. Everything revolves around him. At home, on the street, on horseback, in a carriage. Where did that love and affection go? Clemente is almost always behind the camera, while Gisèle takes care of the boy. But in other photos, he's there, accompanying them. With Eric, or even alone in front of a landscape. Gisèle must have pushed the button sometimes.

As the years pass, there are fewer photos. Especially of Eric. Almost none from his adolescence. Just one or two of him with a ball, playing soccer. That's a time when they start to withdraw, she saw that with Iván.

There are also fewer photos of Gisèle from then. Fewer photos period, as though Clemente's photography and his passion for life were intertwined and at some point all of that began to fade.

In her head, something like a film plays, with scenes from Clemente and Gisèle's life, including snatches of stories he's told her. Marseille, their home, the studio... It's a happy life, like the one on Eric's Facebook. But then, family photos are always happy. She considers the contrast: these photos of life, the others of mourning. In the end, they're about the same thing: that which is no longer there. One may portray happiness and the other sorrow, but both are documents of a present on the verge of extinction.

She looks around more. There are hundreds of negatives. But all of life, none of death. Is that what she's looking for? She goes through all the drawers, and even the closet, and since she's there, the nightstand and under the bed, in search of a box, a clue, something. But all she finds is Clemente's clothes. Folded kerchiefs, underwear, T-shirts... a life she should have left alone. She knows this more the longer she's there, and at last she decides to stop. There must be more, but she's not going to turn the whole house upside down. This isn't research, and she's already delved too far into the secrets of someone who entrusted her with the keys to his house.

There's nothing. She's relieved. Nothing unexpected, nothing to fear.

On her way out, involuntarily, she takes a look around, in case something, some detail in some corner, escaped her notice.

But then she sees it. It was so close she didn't notice. Her heart skips a beat, and she needs to lean on the doorframe to try to take it in.

The window in the back, the curtains, the decoration in the molding, the painting over the bed . . .

She recognizes this room.

She doesn't like using her phone camera, but she snaps a few quick pictures, repeating to herself over and over that she hopes she's wrong. But something tells her she isn't.

VI

THE OTHER SIDE

. . .

IV

THE OTHER SIDE

1

MAYBE IT'S A MIX-UP. CONTEMPORARY HOUSES, they all look the same. This is what she tells herself as she drives home at top speed, stomping on the gas as if she were being chased. Before, she was playing at being detective, but now a real urgency is burning inside her, an unease and an uncertainty that she needs to get free of as soon as she can.

She doesn't even close the garage door before hurrying into the studio and opening the cabinet she had stuffed Clemente's book into to keep it out of sight. The scent of damp wood and developing fluid has gathered there and stings her eyes. She finds it. Her haste dissipates, time stops. She's scared to look at the last page and hesitates. But then she dares to open it. She doesn't even need to take out her phone to compare the photo she took of the room with the daguerreotype on the last page. It's all too clear. He's rearranged the furnishings, the bedclothes, and the curtains. But the place is the same. The plaster molding, the bed, the wooden nightstands, even the small painting over the headboard, an impressionist landscape that reminds her of Cézanne's *Mont Sainte-Victoire*.

She checks the perspective on her phone and on the page. Without realizing it, she took a similar photo, framed the same way, from what is, perhaps, the most logical angle. The biggest difference is in the curtains and the blinds: open in her photo, closed in the daguerreotype, shrouding the room in darkness. It doesn't take long to guess why: a long exposure and the slight fluctuations of natural light would have affected the definition.

Her thoughts flow past in rapid succession. She puts the book down, jumps up, and walks through the house, trying to process what she's learned. The conclusion isn't hard to reach.

She phones Teresa a few minutes later, and though she's struggling to string together her words, she tries to tell her everything. As she does so, it all becomes more real.

"Relax," Teresa tells her, trying to calm her down. "It's horrible. It is. But it's over. It's not in your hands. What would you do? Turn him in to the cops?"

"No. It's not that."

Of course it's not that. What she feels, what hurts, what upsets her. The disappointment. The deceit. Something—she isn't sure. Right now, she isn't sure of anything at all.

"What about his son?"

"I can't get him to respond."

"There must be a way."

Teresa comes up with the idea. Dolores is hesitant at first, but as she hangs up, she thinks there's no loss in trying. She takes a photo of the last page of the book and sends it to Clemente's son on Facebook. Her nerves get the better of her as she does so. It's only later, when she's sitting comfortably on the edge of the sofa with a cup of hot herbal tea and her eyes lost in the nothingness that she imagines Eric opening the file and reading her brief message:

I found this in one of your father's books. Please, I need to talk to you. Here's my number again.

She's afraid of what he'll answer: Mind your own business.

In this instance, she couldn't argue with him.

2

THE RESPONSE SHE FEARED, OR SOMETHING like it, arrives the next day:

Miss, please leave me in peace. I don't know what you're after, sending me that picture.

She's kept her phone in her hands all morning, in the chair behind the counter in her studio, checking the Facebook Messenger app.

When the notification comes and she opens it, she notices the green dot next to Eric's profile. Iván told her that meant the person was online and using the app. This has never happened before. He's there, she can almost feel him. If he called her on the phone, she would hear his breathing.

Dolores writes and apologizes once more for nosing around in his life. As she types, she keeps her eye on the green dot, as if her message only mattered if it arrived in real time. After begging his pardon, she adds, almost despite herself, *You know who that blurry figure is in the photo, don't you?*

He takes a few seconds to respond. They feel eternal. *That image is painful to me.*

Dolores apologizes again. *I really am sorry for all this.* And she is. She knows how uncomfortable this conversation is.

The bright colors and playful appearance of the application cast a bizarre light on their interaction. She keeps her teeth clenched. She doesn't know what to say next. Whether to ask more questions or not say anything at all. Should she really lend credence to some stranger's babbles? She—always fair, always polite—is she really intentionally causing this man pain?

Her fingers write of their own accord, formulating a question that is like the lash of a whip:

Did he poison her?

Immediately:

Who told you that?

She hesitates. Just for a second.

A neighbor... she writes. And again, feeling guided by an outside force, she tells him about the day of the funeral, what Ascensión told her she saw in the funeral home, the vials of poison her cousin said they'd found among his mother's medicines.

She runs on for too long, a whole paragraph, but in her state, she can't think of a way to condense it. Her nerves are making her ramble, and as she continues, she keeps an eye on the green dot, needing to know that Eric is still there; she tells him Clemente has always been good to her, that he rekindled her passion for photography, that he changed her life, that she can't keep living with these doubts, please, she needs to know the truth, she's sorry for insisting, but she just has to know, did he poison her?

She's surprised at herself. For a moment, she barely knows who she is, who this person is who's typing these things on her phone.

For a long time, he doesn't answer. But he's online, and he's seen the message. She sees three gray dots undulating in space like a little wave. He's writing. On it goes. Then he stops. She imagines him in his home in the South of France, responding to an impertinent stranger. The green dot vanishes. User offline. Dolores assumes it's all over. But she stays in her chair, staring at her phone, gripping it in both hands, almost cracking it in two.

A message pops up on the screen:

Look, Miss, I don't know what you've been told, but the only poison is that image itself. It's pure cruelty. That's all you need to know. No one should die like that.

Dolores isn't sure how to respond. The green dot shines brighter. Eric's still there. She's ashamed, ill at ease. She knows she's been pushy. She knows Eric is about to disconnect. For that reason, she can't help telling him about his father. If she tried for weeks to contact him, that's been why, to let him know how Clemente is. *You need to come,* she concludes. And, undecided, she adds, *No one should die like this.*

Right away, he answers: *For me, he died a long time ago.* And then, a few seconds later, *This conversation is over. Please let me get on with my life.*

That's his last message. After he sends it, he logs off. Her response—*A father is always a father*—goes unread. Her words hover in a digital limbo. She can almost hear the message echo. An empty chat, an absence on the other side.

She opens the app several more times throughout the day. Her message remains unread. Hours pass before she admits that this is the last time they'll ever be in touch. It disconcerts her, she can't absorb all that's happened. Not just the conversation, but her attitude, her insistence, the way she wheedled information out of him. She's not like that. She never has been.

But one thing pacifies her: the poison. Striking it from the picture defuses the tension. *The only poison is the image itself,* Eric wrote. That's what it is. Death in real time before her eyes.

It's strange, only once the conversation is over can she see the scene in her mind, as though she'd held it in reserve until she'd found out the answer to something she was scared to know. She meditates on the image:

the blur over the bed, the distorted face, onto which she now projects Gisèle's face. She surprises herself with her ruminations about what she can't see, what lies outside the field of vision: Where was Clemente during the undefined period of time, thirty seconds, ten minutes, two hours, the whole day? She trembles as she imagines him there behind the lens, impassively contemplating death's arrival.

She goes to bed with a bitter taste in her mouth and an invisible burden weighing on her mind. Tongue dry, eyes tired, a sandstorm around her body. She pays no attention to the dark absence settling over her. Its shuddering doesn't matter to her now.

3

THE SOUND OF THE PHONE AWAKENS HER. SHE looks at the time before picking up. Nine thirty in the morning. She's slept in.

"A family has requested your services."

She doesn't know what they're talking about at first. She hasn't adjusted to reality.

"At the Santa Lucía funeral home," the person specifies. "Don Clemente isn't picking up. But I had your number."

She waits before responding. This is the last thing she feels like doing. But she thinks of the family wanting a photo of their loved one and accepts, telling the man this is the last time. It wasn't calculated, it just came out that way:

"I won't be doing it anymore from now on."

He doesn't try to convince her otherwise. He just says all right. As if he expected it, or didn't really care.

The last time. She can't take more death. She's certain of it as she parks her car, goes inside the funeral home, and finds herself alone with a woman's body in the cold chamber. It's freezing, and almost no one's there. No family members come in with her. The son of the deceased says he prefers to wait outside.

"My mother didn't get along well with the neighbors," is the excuse he offers. "That's why there are so few of us."

He told her his mother died at seventy-six years of age. Dolores doesn't know how old Gisèle was when she died, but it must have been around that. She thinks of them as she looks at the woman: of Gisèle, of the photograph. And she speculates about that last moment.

The woman's still body before her makes her ask herself questions. Did Clemente stay with her the whole time? How could he bear it? She doesn't know if she prefers to believe he left her in her room or stayed behind the camera, waiting for death to come.

She remembers an iconic photograph from a famine in the nineties: an emaciated child, naked, defenseless, being stalked by a vulture in an African village. She can't recall the photographer's name. She read that he killed himself a year after receiving the Pulitzer. Perhaps he couldn't bear the weight of that image. Or rather, of the reality behind it.

She imagines Clemente in front of his wife, waiting for death as a vulture waits for live flesh to turn to carrion. In her mind, it's more like a film than a photo. Everything moves except the one thing that actually did move: that vital quiver, Gisèle's body, remains still, superimposed on the room like a blemish.

She tortures herself with these thoughts. They torment her as she stands in the funeral home trying to find the right angle. She pushes aside the wreaths, places the tripod next to the coffin, comes close, backs away... Her body is an automaton, she thinks when she replaces the flowers and realizes she doesn't remember moving them in the first place. She's been there a long time and still hasn't done her job. It's disrespectful. But nobody notices. No one will see it when they look at the photos. She knows, though. And that's enough. And so, though it takes longer, she offers her forgiveness to the deceased in her mind and starts over. If this is the last photo, she should give it all her care. It's a memory. A monument. A thing of value. She tries again. Serene, present, as the situation demands, as she has learned in those months.

When she says her goodbye to the son and the funeral home employee, she's saying goodbye to something else too. She knows what she does is important. But she lacks the strength to go on.

On the way home, she passes Santa Lucía hospital. She's seen this stretch of road in her head all morning, and with it, the opportunity to visit Clemente. She exits and even parks on the long, level stretch in front. Thoughts crowd in on her. Something like rage. If he was here, she'd struggle to control herself. But what would she do, seek explanations, confront him, ask him to his face how he could act like a vulture?

Her knees are quivering. She bites her fingertips. She breathes hard and clenches her jaw. Her body struggles to control itself enough to walk inside. But she can't, however hard she tries. She can't control her body or her mind. So she waits for what seems like forever before restarting her car and heading home. She's not escaping her problems, she's returning to her people, she tells herself. Teresa was right: those aren't her dead. She doesn't have to carry them with her.

She needs to remake her life, she tells herself as she drives, and for her, this morning, with the sun shining in front of her and the December cold slipping through the cracked window, is a journey back. Something has closed forever, she intuits. But she doesn't know very well what.

4

THE NEXT DAY, SHE DEVELOPS THE PICTURES
from the funeral home, aware the whole time that this
is the end. Leave-taking. Mourning. This knowledge
becomes clearer when she takes them to the son of the
deceased. She wants to do everything right until the end.
Just as Clemente taught her.

Clemente... for days, she couldn't stop thinking of
him. Couldn't stop thinking, with unease, that she'd
ducked a responsibility. It's difficult, but she calls Vasil
to find out how he is. Stable, not any better. A recovery
isn't likely.

"He asked about you," Vasil says.

"Tell him I called."

Over the phone, she can hide her dismay. But she
couldn't do it with him in front of her.

The days fly by, but slowly. It hasn't even been that long
since Clemente first called her. Early August—a little

over four months. The blink of an eye, and simultane-
ously a lifetime.

She tries to gather her thoughts. She can't tolerate
more death. She doesn't have the courage or the heart.
But she knows that her strange unrest in these months
has made her feel alive and awake—more so than in the
last ten years. Still, she needs her old life back. She can't
stay away from it. Go back to her life—does that mean
going back to the studio and the long days of waiting in
vain for some client to arrive?

She knows it's a vestige of the past, the last glimpse
of a world that's disappeared. What's the point in keeping it open? When will she finally take the step? It's
been eating at her lately. Next year, maybe. And telling
herself this makes it slowly become a reality.

She announces it at dinner on Christmas Eve when
Teresa asks. Next year, she responds. I decided. And she
leaves it at that. Even if Christmas isn't the best time for
making big decisions. There are memories in that shop,
and closing it hurts her worse than it should. It's where
they celebrated their first Christmas Eve after marrying.
They put a big table in the back and invited the whole
family, renting a backdrop with a snowy landscape on it
and snapping pictures of anyone who would let them. It
was a happy Christmas. The next ones were, too, when
Iván was born and the whole world started revolving
around him. Presents, carols, hopes. It was a time of joy,
a time of looking forward. Then the illness came, and

bitter Christmases followed. The one after her mother's death, with her father frail at home. The one after Luis's death, which she tried to erase from her memory. No dinner, no tree, no nativity scene. She was sorry for Iván, he was just a kid after all, but her mourning got the better of her.

The holidays are when the dead come back to her. She thinks about them more then than she does at any other time of year. The melancholy used to take away her breath; it doesn't anymore. Her sorrow doesn't keep her from sharing others' happiness. The memory of good cheer past overlays the sorrow of the present; the absence comes and goes, peeks out and then hides—you can't say it disappears, it never does, but it doesn't negate everything else. And she lets herself smile and she experiences something like delight. So it is tonight, at Teresa's home. Since she's had no obligations to anyone, she celebrates there, with Iván and her sister-in-law's children. There is a space for recollection there—especially in the toast said for those no longer there—but the dinner is cheerful, togetherness is agreeable, they are celebrating those who are still here, and the feeling is more of gratitude than sorrow.

And yet, something remains to be resolved. As much as she pretends and puts on a good face with the younger ones and laughs at Teresa's jokes and stories. Clemente is still there. He's not her father, he's not her responsibility, she keeps telling herself. But she can't stop thinking of him. She hasn't managed to assimilate that scene that keeps growing in her mind: him behind the camera, patiently awaiting his wife's death. It's the reason she couldn't visit him in the hospital. She isn't sure she could look him in the face. She doesn't know what she'd say. What she does know is she doesn't want it to be the same as with Luis's body. Out of field, absent, opaque in memory. She can't let that happen again. But she's still scared that her anger at what Clemente did could turn outward, spreading through, erasing her affection for him.

This fear emerges powerfully when she gets a call from Vasil a few days later.

"You should come...if you want to say goodbye."

His voice is stern, cutting. She hears reproach in it, resentment at her long silence.

"I'll try," she responds.

"I don't think you get other chance."

5

SHE DIDN'T WANT TO ASK THE ROOM NUMBER.
It would make it too obvious that she hasn't been there in
weeks. She goes to the third floor—she remembers that,
at least—and looks around, confused, sticking her head
into several doors until she finds the right one.

She isn't sure if this is it, but then she sees Vasil in
the corner, spread out in a pleather chair, dressed in a
pajama-like tracksuit and staring at his cell phone screen.
His beard is long, his thin hair matted and greasy. He
looks like a patient too. He smiles when he sees her.
None of the anger she thought she heard on the phone
is evident in his face. He places the back of one hand on
his cheek and bends his head slightly. He means that
Clemente's asleep.

No one else is in there, but the curtain's still pulled,
and they have to come close to see him. A tangle of tubes
and wires connects his body to the respirator. As soon as
she's gotten a look at him, Vasil gestures for her to come
with him.

"Now it's just wait," he says, sighing, outside the door. "I thought you wouldn't come."

It sounds like a reproach. She tries not to hold it against him. He's right.

He tells her the doctor says Clemente may not make it through the day. He's suffocating, and his organs have started to fail. Vasil's face is strained, and he's hurting, he looks as if he were talking about his own son. She can tell how much he cares for him, and doesn't know how to console him. She rests a hand on his shoulder and frowns.

"Go have something in the cafeteria and relax a minute," she says. "I'll stay with him till you get back."

Vasil thanks her and goes back in to retrieve his phone and his wallet. When he's left, Dolores pulls a chair over to Clemente's bed and settles in quietly. At last, she can observe him. He's shrunken since the last time she saw him. He reminds her of her father. He, too, shrunk as the days passed, burning out, disappearing, age and illness consuming what was left of him.

She watches and listens. The constant beeping of the machine, the labored breath. A snore like a death rattle. She watched her father die. She can't forget it. There was a click, and the rhythm of his breathing changed, his body shifted planes, respiration rougher, choppy, the cadence dull and shallow and slowly going dead. Clemente isn't making that sound yet. His noise is an echo of life, the throb of a sleeping body. But she knows that soon, that final gasp will come, the air will stop circulating, the body will be vacated.

A few minutes later, Clemente opens his eyes, and they look at each other. He tries to talk, but his voice fails him. His expression and his guttural murmur faintly evoke the word *thanks*.

Dolores smiles, attempting to control herself. She doesn't want to think of the picture in the book. That scene she never saw, but has imagined, returns to her, that unquiet figure in the photo, Clemente observing the horror behind the camera.

Unable to escape these thoughts, Dolores takes his hand. When her father died, she held his hand till the end. She remembers that endless night. For a long time, she retained the trace of him on her skin, how tightly he held her, as if he were gripping the anchor, the handhold of life.

It's still there, lodged in her memory. The sorrow, the grief, the satisfaction of spending that last moment at his side. Gisèle didn't get that, she tells herself. She died alone. Without her pillar, without a hand to hold, with Clemente distant, looking and looked at, on the wrong side. This is how she conceives of it: on the wrong side. In the distance. The image that kills. The touch that saves.

She comes a bit closer, squeezes his hand, shakes it softly.

"Here," she whispers. "Near you. Not on the other side, far away."

She says nothing more. But she feels the old man squeeze her back. And she sees his tears slipping down under the oxygen mask. She thinks he's understood the meaning of her words. She can guess at all that's passing through his mind.

She feels their bodies talking. Their gestures, their intertwined hands, their fingers. Saying all the things she doesn't know how to put in words. All she'd like to say. Phrases that don't come, condensed on the skin, in the slight pressure of the fingers, life incarnate, protecting, accompanying.

She isn't sure how long they spend that way. Time stopped, and it only starts to move again when Vasil comes through the door. Dolores looks at him and holds Clemente's hand a few more minutes, not letting go until she decides to leave.

Well before coming, she knew she wouldn't wait until it was over. She's not ready to repeat that experience. And Vasil is with him. The closest thing to his son.

"Hold his hand when the end comes," she whispers in his ear. "That's all I ask of you."

She doesn't say goodbye. It would sound too conclusive. She kisses Clemente on the forehead and squeezes his hand one last time. She hugs Vasil, holding back tears.

She turns on her way out of the room. What she sees is not a stationary scene. Life goes on there. Touch has won the battle. The image will come when the body stops pulsing and all that's left is memory. But for now, it's holding on. And its movement, muffled, tenuous, is worth more than any photograph.

EPILOGUE

OCHRE SEA OVER GRAY SKY. WATER ABOVE, SUS-pended on a plane of dense air that expands through space like an opaque cloud. That's what she sees through the viewfinder. The image inverted. Abstract surfaces of color, lines traced on the horizon. A Rothko in turbid tones, inverted.

She's come out early to photograph the sea. After a week, the rain has let up. The third flood in less than four months. Gloria, a funny name for a storm. Everyone thought it would pass them by. It wouldn't happen again. It couldn't. But the storm crossed half the globe to lash the village. A few last bursts before it lifts, the media said. But in fact, it had been a cruel blow destroying things that had struggled to get back off the ground.

Everything is mud. Again. The ochre water of the fields has crossed the village and drained into the sea. The clay soil stains the roads and clouds the soul, and the mood is gray and muted. Everything happens again. An infinite cycle. And beneath that repetition of

ever-more-frequent catastrophes, there's the sense that
the world is crumbling. Dolores feels it this morning at
the end of January, unable to escape the cold and the
damp. The air is heavy, the colors are despairing, you
can almost taste the iron in the clay.

She's attached the bellows camera to the tripod on
the sand. The sun's rising, and the beach is a desert. The
fallen blocks from the esplanade have yet to be replaced.
Far away, she can hear the hum of the diggers. The
workers are beginning to rebuild. On the shore, a gull
searches in vain for food. There are no dying fish there.
Not yet. But they'll be there soon, she thinks. Everything is below the surface for now. The sun is posing for
the picture. But something grim is throbbing beneath it,
buried under that brown blanket that turns greenish as it
recedes into the distance.

She needs to record this. After the news, the photos in the papers, the videos that keep appearing on her
phone...she needs to capture that thing that supposedly
can't be captured. Fix that light on the silvered plate. So
nothing will be forgotten, nothing lost.

Last night, while she was gathering her equipment for
the daguerreotype, she remembered Clemente. Everything was there lying on the table in the lab just as
she had left it three weeks before. That day, too, she
felt an obligation. She'd promised herself she wouldn't

photograph the dead again. But when Vasil called her, she needed to shoot that last image. For Clemente, but also for her. She was shocked by that demand rising up inside her to keep forever a thing that would soon cease to be visible.

Promises are there to be broken, she told herself, so new promises can take their place. And on that third day of the new year, without even bothering to get dressed, she carefully prepared a copper plate, slipped it into its frame, and readied the bellows camera. Before going out, she sent a message to Clemente's son: *Your father died this morning. I'm just writing to let you know. I'm very sorry.*

He still hadn't read the previous message. She shouldn't have bothered him again. He'd told her that for him, his father was already dead, and had been for a long time. But it seemed like the right thing to do. And doing it put her unexpectedly at ease.

She got into the car, still feeling calm, and left for the funeral home on that wintry Friday. Along the way, she saw that something was coming to an end. And it became clearer when she saw Vasil and hugged him and he sobbed. She was silent as she tried to imagine what she was feeling. Not sorrow, not despair. Grief, of course, sadness at the loss of a friend. But there was something else more complex, a sense of peace, a sense that things were as they should be.

This impression strengthened as she stood alone in the cold chamber with the body. The face. Sharp features. Groomed beard. Him, again. Old, but not de-crepit. Elegant, though they hadn't dressed him in one of his suits. A white satin cloth covered him. He wouldn't have cared for that, she thought.

She didn't break down. She remembered her shell, the cold, stony membrane over her heart. She wondered if it had returned. But she didn't feel remoteness, she felt quietude, a silent satisfaction. She couldn't grasp it, but she could feel it: something physical settling in her, as a dislocated bone settles in its socket. A weight falling from her back. She could even hear the popping in her vertebrae as she opened the tripod and placed the camera close to the coffin.

She looked at his face again. It was all she wanted to capture. The face in the foreground. Everything else was superfluous. She tried, without meaning to, to find the same angle as in that blurred portrait she took the day he spoke to her of the unquiet ones. *I'm not yet dead*, he told her then. Now he was. And she trusted the result-ing picture would be clear. A perfect effigy, life made stationary.

She patiently waited for the exposure. Forty seconds. A little long. The lighting wasn't bad, but she wanted to be sure the image would settle on the plate.

While the photo was being made—this is how she thought of it, as something being made, as if by na-ture, with her there as an intercessor between reality and its double—that sense of physical ease deepened, and it struck her that in that image all the others were encapsulated, all those lifeless bodies, even the one she couldn't force herself to look at. The absent image that had accompanied her the last ten years, the dark void that stalked her and hummed around her. And for reasons she couldn't plumb, that emptiness began to vanish, as though Clemente's body were a strange attractor, a magnetic field absorbing guilt and dissolving it. This was how she thought of it. Clemente's lifeless body was the body of all those who were no longer there. This was, perhaps, the origin of that odd composure, that notion that something had finally found its place.

She didn't stay for the cremation. Something else was burning in her backpack: the image eating its way into the plate, that final reflection in the mirror. Why did she take just one daguerreotype? Why didn't she take other photos to preserve his memory? She didn't think about it. It may be she only wanted one. That was all. The last trace of light on a body. A relic.

The image appeared clearly: a fine silhouette, slowly taking on definition. It wasn't perfect. But it was the best daguerreotype she'd done. Luminous. The bright white of the satin sheet. The soft shadows in his white beard. The limpid face. Haggard, but his. The man who generously and gently observed her photos and spoke words no one had uttered to her in ages and woke something that had been dormant for many years. She couldn't forget that this same face had, at the decisive moment, chosen to remain on the other side of the camera. The wrong side, as he realized—or so she likes to think—when she was there squeezing his hand. The one that wept in thanks for that gesture, and for her clemency. The very same one. What endured of him. What was left, all that was left.

Only once she had the plate in her hand, exuding a corporeal warmth, could Dolores cry for Clemente. In the hospital, she'd told him it was better to be close than far away, and had grasped that touch is salvation, the image death. But later, she saw that the image, too, could be salvation, that when the body is gone, we have no choice but to be far away. And the image brings us close, is a trace that helps us abide in the distance even as it undergirds it. She understood. Images calm, cauterize the wound, give form to the emptiness, name it, make it visible, and at the same time protect from it, even trap it.

She arrived at this certainty the afternoon she finished the daguerreotype and sheltered it behind a thin sheet of glass. And she promised herself then she would take photographs again, build a link in that tradition that would help others give shape to the void. As Clemente had done his entire life, as she had learned to do.

Not long afterward, Vasil told her Clemente had bequeathed her his collection. She wouldn't get the official notice until a few weeks later, probably, but he'd been there when the old man signed his testament, and he thought it best she not be taken by surprise.

"You should think about what to do with it," he said.

Dolores thanked him, and wondered how best to use that priceless inheritance.

Two weeks have passed now, and she still hasn't decided. It's an honor, a source of pride, to be custodian to that tradition, but she doesn't know if she'll be able to do it properly. What she does know is she won't cede it to the archive. She'll never give Alfonso the satisfaction.

She's thought of turning the studio into a small museum. With Clemente's collection, Luis's photos, and her own. Iván likes the idea, and offered to help if it was what she chose. It would allow her to keep the space and turn it into a memorial. For herself, and also for the village.

She might do it, but for now it's just speculation. She's still waiting to be notified, and doesn't know when she will or what all will be involved. The time will come, and she'll figure out a solution.

Today, in the morning, at the end of January 2020, after several days of rain and the grim return of the floods, she has other things on her mind. She looks at the sea through the lens and sees the image inverted: the sky on the ground, the water a menacing brown cloud. The absence is no longer beside her. It's gone, after all those years. Uncertainty is there, but absence, no. An uncertainty birthed by this calm surface after the storm. A calm that precedes another imminent disaster.

She tries to capture it, and it takes a long time to appear on the copper plate. The placidity that conceals terror. The invisible. The dense air swallowing everything. And something more tenuous than air. A fragile world cracking and crumbling to pieces. Everything under that calm, small sea.

She doesn't know what will happen when the rains return, when disaster comes, when the world falls apart again. All she can say for certain is that whatever lies in store, she'll know how to face it. She has no doubts, she thinks, as the day comes to its end, and she places the daguerreotype of the still sea in a vitrine beside the one of the old man's inert face: life stops, but sooner or later, it always moves forward again. And this time, she's sure, as she is of few other things, that she won't be left behind.

This is clearer to her than ever as she inhales through her nose, feels the air invade her body and touch the bottom of her lungs. There is nothing left that can stop her from breathing.

ACKNOWLEDGMENTS

NO ONE WRITES ALONE, AND THIS BOOK IS NO exception. As I was putting together *Anoxia*, I was fortunate enough to have the valuable assistance of people I feel obliged to mention here.

For their observations and suggestions, thanks to Manuel Moyano, Leonardo Cano, Diego Sánchez Aguilar, Silvia Pérez, Antonio Candeloro, Mercedes Alarcón, and, of course, Raquel Alarcón, my first reader. Their wise comments and advice substantially improved this novel, as did Marina Penalva and Silvia Sesé with their reading, companionship, and trust. Nor can I forget my conversations with Fernando Vázquez and Asensio Martínez about the tradition of mortuary photography. Though I consulted numerous texts on the subject, I would like to mention the essential works of Jay Ruby (*Secure the Shadow: Death and Photography in America*, Cambridge, Mass., MIT Press, 1995) and Virginia de la Cruz Lichet (*El retrato y la muerte. La tradición de la fotografía post mortem en España*, Madrid,

Temporae, 2013, and *Post Mortem. Collectio Carlos Areces*, Madrid, Titilante Ediciones, 2021). I owe a special debt to Hélène Védrenne and Nina Zaragoza for showing me the magic of the daguerreotype and giving me a glimpse of the secrets of their workshop in Jávea, as well as to Paco Gómez for his meticulous assistance with photographic techniques and materials. Last of all, I cannot avoid thanking from the bottom of my heart my friends and neighbors from the villages of the Mar Menor. Their endurance, firmness, and steadfastness in the face of the disasters—some natural, some provoked by human action—that have devastated and continue to devastate their homes and their environment have been a source of inspiration for this book. May their spirit never flag, and may their fight never cease.

ABOUT THE AUTHOR

MIGUEL ÁNGEL HERNÁNDEZ is a Spanish writer best known for his works of fiction, among them the novels *Intento de escapada* (2013), which won the Premio Ciudad Alcalá de Narrativa and was translated into five languages, *El instante de peligro* (2015), which was a finalist for the Premio Herralde de Novela, and *El dolor de los demás* (2018), which was selected as a book of the year by *El País* and the *New York Times en Español*. Hernández teaches art history at the University of Murcia and has authored several books on art and visual culture.

ABOUT THE TRANSLATOR

ADRIAN NATHAN WEST is a writer and literary critic based in Spain. He has translated more than twenty books, among them Sergio Pàmies's *The Art of Wearing a Trench Coat* (Other Press, 2021), Sibylle Lacan's *A Father: Puzzle*, and Rainald Goetz's *Insane*.